A Bi Bouquet

letters from Myrtle

For Aandie,
Best wishes,
Sherry Boone

by

Sherry W. Boone

Proverbs 17:22

Available from:
Parkway Publishers, Inc.
P. O. Box 3678
Boone, North Carolina 28607
Telephone/Facsimile: (828) 265-3993

www.parkwaypublishers.com

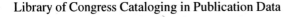

Library of Congress Cataloging in Publication Data

Boone, Sherry W.
  A bloomin' bouquet : letters from Myrtle / by Sherry W. Boone.
  p. cm.
  ISBN 1-887905-81-2
  1. North Carolina--Social life and customs--Fiction. 2. Appalachian Region,
Southern--Fiction. 3. Mountain life--Fiction. I. Title.

  PS3602.O658B58 2003
  813'.6--dc22
   2003022434

Editing, Layout and Book Design: Julie Shissler
Cover Design: Aaron Burleson, Spokesmedia

This book is dedicated to my late maternal grandparents,
Esta Lee and Creed Morgan and their seven daughters.
My aunts Hazel, Ruth, Frieda, Louise, Maxine and Carolyn
were all-important figures in my life. Delilah, my mother,
passed the family values and love for God that had been instilled
in her to me. Grandma and Grandpa, Louise and my mother
are no longer living but their memories are precious
and very much alive.

Without Sam Boone, my late husband, I would have had
very little inspiration for "Letters from Myrtle."
He gave me love, many laughs and "heart tickles."

I am grateful for my family and for the friends who nudged me
along to write this book. You know who you are. Thank you.

About the Book

Reading these wonderful pieces is just like sitting on the porch and sipping iced tea with a friend—wise, warm, and funny, Sherry Boone is the best company in the world.

Lee Smith

Sherry Boone is a captivating writer and storyteller. No one can read or hear her stories and not be touched deeply. How fortunate we all are that she is willing to share her words with us. I wish only that she would keep writing for many years to come.

Virginia Foxx

From her entertaining, enlightening and inspiring columns, Sherry Boone has taken the printed word to a higher level, sharing it with her many fans in "Letters from Myrtle." I have always enjoyed Sherry's commentary, whether it tells the stories of angels or the pain of losing a loved one, she is a storyteller and writer worth hearing and reading. Her style is so at ease, it's like sitting on a couch and talking with a close friend. She comes into your home via the radio or the newspaper, and you just don't want her to leave.

Sandy Shook, News Production Editor, The Watauga Democrat

I believe Sherry Boone's heart beats with compassion for every human being on earth. These stories of the everyday foibles of family, friends and neighbors are told with love and irresistible good humor. I have laughed and cried for over a decade by reading and rereading what Miss Myrtle has to report.

Alice Phoebe Naylor, Director, Doctoral Program in Educational Leadership, Appalachian State University, Boone, NC.

I've had the pleasure of knowing and working with "Myrtle" for several years. Sherry has read her "Letters From Myrtle" on the air at WECR and they have become a popular portion of my morning show. She never fails to make me laugh, and sometimes even brings a tear."Myrtle's" humorous and touching outlook on life shines through in each letter, both entertaining the listener and providing a reminder of the truly important things in life. Sherry, I appreciate what you and "Myrtle" have brought to my program and listeners, and to me also.

Bill Fisher, WECR-FM, Boone, NC.

Sherry Boone, with her "just talking to you" style, makes you feel as comfortable as though you were listening to your best friend confiding secrets. The beauty of this mountain area and its people shines through each scene as these stories from her heart celebrate the joy, wisdom, and foolishness she finds sparkling in everyday mountain life.

These stories touch your heart and tickle the funny bone as they come to life with believable characters going about their delightful daily adventures. Sherry's warmth, enthusiasm, compassion, and love of people and their foibles make you say, "Yes!" to life.

Dianne Hackworth, storyteller, Todd, NC.

About the Author

Sherry W. Boone realized that she was a writer after she became a grandmother. A Christmas play was her first attempt at writing, starting a chain reaction that hasn't let up. She has her own column "Blue Ridge View" which appears in the Watauga Democrat.

"Letters from Myrtle" were first written to lift the spirits of shut-ins via homemade cassettes. Many people have had the opportunity since then to read the stories in local newspapers and hear them aired on local radio and National Public Radio.

Sherry lives in the Blue Ridge Mountains of North Carolina. She and her late husband Sam were the parents of three children and grandparents of six.

Contents

A Trace of Tar

Dear Hazel,

Can you believe it? Me and Barney's movin' back to North Carolina after livin' in the Sunshine State for 17 years! We're gonna live in the mountains in a camper 'til we can put up a buildin' which will house a little country store for us to run and an apartment in which we can abide.

I'm so excited I can't sleep. Here I am 40 years old and so many plans are in the makin'. First of all, we're gettin' a grandbaby, changin' careers, movin' to a new location where everybody's gonna be strangers, and last but not least, our silver anniversary is comin' up this summer.

Which reminds me, do you ever run in to Penelope Wagner? I'd just love for her to know that me and Barney's still married and that my heart still tickles when he smiles at me. You probably don't know this but she made the remark after our marriage that she'd give it three months to last 'cause Barney was so fickle! If you should see her, how's 'bout droppin' us into the conversation somehow.

I don't think I've been so happy and sad at the same time since me and Barney eloped. I was happy to be Barney's bride, but sad 'cause I slipped off to marry him without tellin' my mama. Well, in one way, history is repeatin' itself. I'm happy to be goin' but sad to be leavin' our girls down here in South Florida. B.J. (that's what we call Barney, Jr. now) lives near Charlotte so we'll be closer to him and his wife but so far away from our girls. You might say that we're leavin' the nest and I feel just a tad guilty.

We still have some tar on our heels. I'm eager to get back nearer to my birthplace. Barney's eager to get back to the land of Richard Petty and car racin'. Richard's one of his favorite people. I like him too, but not as much as Barney does.

I'll drop you a letter when we get settled. If you don't mind, you might say a prayer or two for me. I feel like they might come in handy.

Love,
Myrtle

A Movin' Experience

Greetin's from North Carolina to my darlin' daughters,

The puffy has gone down on my eyes so I will try to write and tell you 'bout our trip here.

In the first place, Yvonne, I made a bad mistake when I asked you and Camille to come over when we left. But I wanted us to be together as a family as long as we could. And since B. J. had come down to help us drive, I thought the idea was a good one. Wrong.

I felt like a gypsy in a funeral procession. There was your Dad in the U-Haul, B. J. in the van and me in the old blue Plymouth all packed to the gills pullin' out on our trek back to North Carolina.

I might have done all right if you hadn't said what you did, Yvonne. When you put your arms around me to say good-bye and I latched on to you like I'd never see you again, did you have to say," I'll see you in the mornin', Mama?"

My heart flat broke in two 'cause it'll be many mornin's before we can see each other again. You couldn't say good-bye, could you, honey? I hate goodbyes. They seem so permanent. But I promise that I'll be there when the baby's born. We can look forward to that. And you've got your sissy there so everything will be fine. I know it will.

Girls, do you realize that your dad would never let me drive on a trip before? I think he let me drive this time 'cause he wasn't gonna be ridin' in the car with me.

I looked in the rearview mirror and saw you girls wavin' till we was outta sight. I felt like drivin' around the block and right back again to say," I've changed my mind, I'm stayin." But I couldn't do that, now could I? It seemed like God said, "Calm down, Myrtle. You've got to drive a long way tonight. I'm right here beside you. You're not alone in this car."

I tried to stop cryin' but couldn't. I'd get control of myself and then here'd come that picture — in my mind —of ya'll wavin' again.

I tried to sing but it's not possible to sing and cry, at the same time, I found out. Do you remember that song about catchin' a fallin' star and puttin' it in your pocket? Well, thank goodness, I could sing that one without cryin' so I did, all the way to Georgia.

We was in Georgia makin' good time when your Dad took a wrong turn and was headed due west. By the time I realized we was goin' in the wrong direction, we had traveled twenty miles or so. I blowed the horn and blinked my lights but I couldn't get his attention.

I know full well that he was listenin' to Waylon and Willie or somebody on that country station with it blarin' out so loud he couldn't hear.

We was in a no passin' zone but I eased over to where I could see around him and that no one was meetin' us. I pulled back behind your Dad and motioned for B.J. to pass us. I figured that would get your Dad's attention and get him back into the real world.

I could have done it but your brother's had more practice in reckless drivin' than me. I did do my part though. I prayed for his safety. I also started watchin' the road signs better.

We drove straight through to North Carolina and was dead tired the next day when we pulled into B. J.'s yard. In fact, I've never been as tired in my life. Thank goodness, we already had the camper set up ahead of time on our mountain property. All's we had to do was drive from Mecklenburg County to Watauga County the next day to find a storage place for our furniture. But that trip was a pleasant one compared to the hundreds of miles we had traveled earlier.

I know why grandma loves "her mountains" so much. I feel like they're steppin' stones into heaven! Now she'll be able to come up here and enjoy 'em anytime she wants too. Bless her heart.

Girls, I miss you both but I have the most serene feelin' that everything's right in my world. It's been a long time since I felt that way. I can almost feel God's hand on my shoulder. Besides, I know He rode in the car with me from Florida so I shouldn't be surprised to feel His presence now, should I?

And wait 'til I tell you where we stored our furniture. He had a hand in that too. It'll have to wait though since I must write two more letters before I go to bed.

I'll be writin' more letters than that Abby girl in the paper bein's we won't have a phone for a while.

But I promise to keep you up-to-date on our progress.

How have you been feelin', Yvonne? Does the baby move a lot? Sing to it so's it'll know it's loved just as I love the both of you.

Mama

A Place of Refuge

Hello my darlin' daughters,

Sorry about all the cards I've been sendin' but writin' time's scarce as hen's teeth around here. But I promised I'd write to tell you what we did with our furniture.

Young'uns, we couldn't find a place to rent to store our furniture. We rode all over this end of the county and trust me when I say there wasn't a single place available out here in the boondocks. It's a far cry from livin' in town.

Well, I said, "Lord, could You please let us in on Your plans for us? I know You wanted us to move here but You've got to be a little more specific, if You don't mind, if You want us to stay. That U-Haul's gotta be unloaded by tomorrow." Of course, He knew that but I figured I'd remind Him anyways.

About then I noticed a little white church sittin' off the side of the road—up on a hill and the front door was ajar. "Look, Barney," I said "somebody's in that church 'cause the door's open. Let's go see if they can help us find a place."

"Don't see no car around but it's pretty up there. We'll stop," he said.

Pretty wasn't the word for it. The church was nestled under huge oak trees and a creek was runnin' out back with big boulders in it, and you could cross the creek without gettin' your feet wet.

A baptismal pool was located at the edge of the cemetery next to the creek. Just about every church out here has it's own little cemetery. I'm tellin' you I can't get over the difference between country and city livin'. Cows was grazin' all around outside the church yard and across the road. This was a country church if there's ever been one and I loved it.

We went inside and called out to anyone that might have been there but no one answered. We was all alone in the church—well, except for God. Somebody had picked a vase full of beautiful flowers and put 'em on a table located down in front of the altar.

I sat down on a pew about half way towards the front and could hear the creek as it rushed along makin' its way to the river.

Girls, have you ever took time to just sit and listen to nature? A bird was just a-chirpin' and all that was goin' on right then made me want to cry. Not because I was sad but 'cause I was glad—glad to have a Creator that loved us enough to think to give us such pleasures in life. And one that wouldn't take 'em away if we didn't 'preciate 'em.

When we was ready to leave your dad said, "Do you think we should shut the door or leave it open like we found it?"

"We should shut it," I answered. I think the door was left open for us so's we could go in to get a blessin'—one we was in need of.

Anyways, after we left the church, we hadn't gone but a short distance when we noticed a young couple standin' in their yard talkin' to a woman. "I'm gonna stop and talk to that man," your dad said. He told me to stay put in the car and I did while he moseyed over to 'em.

Right off the bat they was smilin' and shakin' hands and then they all looked real serious like they was listenin' to a sad story or somethin'. Then the smiles come back and the young woman looked my way and waved and then the hand shakin' started all over again and your dad scurried back to the car and was singin' "What A Friend We Have In Jesus" when he cranked up the Plymouth. The couple waved till we was out of sight and I said, "What in the world was all that shakin' and wavin' about?" (The people up here do an awful lot of wavin' and I love it. It makes me feel like they're sayin' "Hey, Myrtle, we're so glad you're here—welcome.")

"You might say that we was makin' an agreement about storin' our furniture and shakin' on it," your dad said.

"Oh, good. They know where there's a place for rent. Thank the Lord," I shouted. But they didn't know of a place for rent. Instead, they told your dad that we could put our belongin's in their basement for as long as need be. And get this, girls—they didn't live in the house where we saw 'em. They live in Tennessee and was visitin' friends that lived where we saw 'em. Can you believe that? I hope you can, 'cause that's precisely the way it happened.

We're real close to the Tennessee line and to where the couple abides. And they even helped us unload the furniture when we took it to their house.

I know that God sent us to that couple in our time of need. We didn't know 'em from Adam and they never laid eyes on us before, but God knew us all and had it planned out ahead of time.

I'm proud to say that we've made our first mountain friends.

I could go on and on but I must stop so I can write to Bernice. Have you talked to her lately, Yvonne? You girls take care of each other.

I'll write agin soon.
Love, Mama

Down in the Dumps

Dear Hazel,

Thanks for the anniversary card. Twenty-five years of wedded bliss. Well, most of 'em's been blissful but there has been some aggravations, most of which has come while we've been cramped up in this dadburn camper all summer. The romance has done gone out the camper window and temper's has been flarin' just a tad lately.

The buildin's 'bout finished now so we'll be movin' in the apartment soon. Barney wasn't no dummy when he decided for us to live in this camper for a while. He knew I'd be so happy to get moved into the apartment I'd forget the big house we sold with all them bathrooms and space to move around in without bumpin' into each other. He's a smart man—my Barney.

However, he wasn't so smart last week when we was on our way to visit B.J. and Dil. Dil's real name is Marianna Elizabeth but that's too long a name for me to call her so I call her Dil for short. That stands for daughter-in law.

I'll start at the beginning when Barney said, "Myrtle, let's drop off garbage on the way to B.J.'s."

We don't have garbage pickups like you city slickers do. We have to carry ours to dumpsters and the county hauls it off when the dumpsters are full and runnin' over.

"Fine," I said. Nothin' like ridin' in a van with the smell of garbage floatin' around. Anyways, I got this bright idea to take our dirty laundry with us so's we could wash it at B.J.'s while we visited. The creek water has lost its pioneer charm somehow. It's not nearly as much fun to catch and use to wash the laundry as it once was.

As I was sayin', I gathered up the laundry and since I didn't have nothin' to put it in, I stuffed it in a garbage bag and put my box of Tide on top and placed it in the back of the van but away from the other bags, of course.

In that bag was my brand new muumuu. I hadn't even wore it. In fact, I was savin' it to wear on the eve of our anniversary for Barney, if you know what I mean.

That muumuu was lovely with big hibiscus all over it and I had got it for a real bargain on a blue light special at K-Mart, and had pictured myself wearin' it many times—in my mind.

Barney would be sittin' out by the campfire and he'd say, "Come out here, Myrtle and watch the sunset with me." I'd get to the camper door and pause for a second or two to let the breeze softly brush the hem against my ankles (kinda like Loretta Young used to do before she'd make her entrance into the room in the openin' of her television show).

You may not remember Loretta Young doin' this but I do and she always looked so lovely and like I said, I had it all planned out — in my mind—to do the same thing but it wasn't meant to be.

Because I wanted that muumuu to feel soft and cuddly, I throwed it in with the laundry so's I could wash it before I wore it. And Barney throwed it away before he got the chance to enjoy it, bless his heart. It makes me sick just thinkin' 'bout it.

I say he throwed it away and he did, but I was at fault too. While he was unloadin' the garbage I was sittin' in the van watchin' the hang gliders soarin' up above Tater Hill when something said, "You'd better get back there, Myrtle, and make sure Barney don't throw the laundry away."

But did I listen? No! I sat there like a dummy watchin' them hang gliders.

Anyways, after we got to B.J.'s, I said, "Barney darlin', would you please bring in my bag of laundry so's I can wash clothes while we're here?"

He said, "What laundry?"

Hazel, it hit me like a bolt outta the blue. I was warned and didn't listen. I can't believe I was so caught up in watchin' and failed to listen. I admit I grieved 'bout our loss and it was a big loss too. The muumuu wasn't the only new thing in that bag. I'd bought towels and jeans and all kinds of things before we moved 'cause I knew it'd be a while before I'd have money for shoppin'—not 'til we was opened for business and makin' a livin' again. I hope somebody found them things and salvaged 'em before the truck got to 'em and hauled 'em to the landfill.

Every time I drive into town I expect to see my muumuu hangin' on a clothesline somewhere flappin' in the breeze. I hope it's givin' some sweet couple the pleasure it was gonna give me and my Barney.

Come see us sometime—preferably after we get moved into our apartment. We'll be glad to have you.

Love,
Myrtle

Up Above the Clouds

Howdy Bernice,

    I just wish you was here with me right this very minute. I'm sittin' up at the top of our property all by myself—well, God's with me of course. I'll try to paint you a picture of what I'm lookin' at.

    Our camper is out of sight because the trees block my view. Picture a mountain covered with daisies and little purple flowers. Humming birds are dartin' all over the place. And the little creek is gurglin' as the water rushes down the mountain past the camper.

    Now across the highway I can see a white cloud that's sittin' lower than the top of the mountain. Can you believe that? I never knew that clouds could do that, did you? But they can. That mountain is wearing a white crown. The green peak is pokin' right through the crown like the lady's head on the Statue of Liberty.

    You'd love the mountains, Bernice. We could have so much fun together pickin' blackberries. The bushes are loaded with berries. I picked a gallon of 'em yesterday and was on my way back down to the camper when I seen the longest black snake I ever seen in my life. That snake was stretched out and musta been five feet long. I said to myself, "What would Bernice do in a case like this? She'd look the other way and pretend she didn't see it and go on about her business. That's what she'd do." But Bernice, I couldn't do that, honey. I screamed at the top of my lungs and prayed, "Heavenly Father, give me the power to out run that snake", and I took off to runnin' as fast as my feet would go. I don't know what become of the snake. Have you ever tried to run downhill? No, I guess not, since you've been in South Florida all your life.

    Well, the harder you run, the faster you go, even a tad faster than you want to go. Bernice, I couldn't stop and them berries was gettin' slung all over the place. My feet flew out from under me or I'd still be movin' on, I reckon. All's I had left of the berries was just enough to put in a little bowl for Barney to eat on his cereal. He said, "You was gone long enough to pick more berries than this, Myrtle. What was you doin' all that time up on the mountain?" I told him I was just relaxin' and enjoyin' nature but I didn't mention the snake. He has a strange sense of humor, and that was not a laughin' matter. I bet you didn't laugh when you just read about that snake, now did you? I bet you said, "Myrtle, sugar, that snake wouldn't hurt you. But you could have hurt yourself. You've got to be more careful."

I miss you, Bernice. I miss our talks. I need to make some friends. I can count my mountain friends on one hand and that's countin' the mailman. I'm lonesome. Barney's workin' so hard to get us in that buildin' so's we can start makin' a livin' again. Bless his heart, he don't hardly have time to talk to me. And you know how I love to talk.

It's scary thinkin' about our store since we never done that kind of work before and we don't know no people to speak of yet. That's what really bothers me. What if these folks don't like us and won't give us their business? What in the world will we do then? That store's not even built yet and I'm already worryin' about it.

I'm givin' this problem to God. I can't worry about this right now. Besides, if He can make such a beautiful crown for that mountain over there, He can sure take care of me and Barney, now can't He?

Well, Bernice, I feel like we just had a visit—you and me. Remember, we're friends forever.

Love,
Myrtle

P.S. Are my girls doin' okay? I got the post card from you. Write a letter when you can.

Company's Comin'

Dear Hazel,

I got your letter and was pleased as punch to hear you're comin' up to see us. Will that be for a day or what?

It's not that I don't want you to come. I do. It's just that the camper's so tiny and crowded. In fact, when we first got here I said to my Barney, "This is like bein' on a second honeymoon. It's more cozy than crowded." But the longer we're in it it's becomin' more crowded than cozy, if you know what I mean.

How's the weather in Charlotte? I do hope it's not as hot as it is here. This camper feels like a roaster oven with the temperature set on high in the daytime. However, it's cold at night and I 'bout freeze to death. So be sure and bring a pair of shorts and a coat.

On top of all that, we've got mice! I knew somethin' was inside the camper that belonged outside when every night I'd hear it rovin' around inside the walls when I couldn't sleep because of all the racket goin' on out in the woods around the camper. The hoot owls and bobcats hoot and scream all night long soundin' just like people in misery. You might want to bring some sleepin' pills too and some ear plugs.

I shut the windows to keep out the cold and the smell of the polecats but it don't do a bit of good.

Anyways, getting back to the mice. We discovered it was a mouse instead of a snake crawlin' around when me and Barney was sittin' down at the table playin' a game of cards. I think it was Old Maid.

Low and behold, a mouse run across the table causin' me to scream and throw my cards up in the air. Burnt me up too, 'cause I had the Old Maid and Barney was just about ready to pluck her outta my hand.

"Calm down, Myrtle. That mouse is more scared of you than you are of it," Barney said. But he was wrong. Then he said," I'll take my shower and we'll play another game of cards later.

Just as soon as he got out of the shower, I hopped in and had no sooner got wet when the camper commenced to rockin' back and forth with such a force that I immediately started prayin' for our safety. I knew for sure that a funnel cloud had touched down and we was about to be relocated.

I grabbed a towel so's I'd be decent when my body was found and opened the bathroom door in time to see Barney jumpin' around in his "Fruit of the Looms" tryin' to dodge that mouse that had tried its best to run up his leg.

But don't worry none about that mouse 'cause we caught it in a trap and the next night we caught its mama and papa too. But I must mention that they're from a big family like us and there's lots of survivors.

You don't need to let me know when you're comin'. I'll just look for you when I see you.

Love,
Myrtle

Barney's Place

Bernice,

Lord, how I need to talk to you. I don't know what I'm gonna do. Well, let me hurry and start at the beginnin'.

Do you remember I wrote you we was gonna have a little country store with a section to serve our customers coffee and doughnuts while they was in doin' their shoppin'?

Well, there's been a change in our plans due to the lack of money! Bernice, we've spent so much on the buildin' that we won't be able to buy enough inventory to stock a store so Barney said that we should open up a little cafe and run it till we can stock a store and you know that I have always said that I could never be a waitress or even a cook if I was tryin' to do it for a livin' and now he expects me to help him make us a livin' feedin' a bunch of strangers three meals a day like they was company or somethin'. Don't that beat all?

Just when I thought I could sit back and relax and enjoy mountain livin' while I worked part-time in our store, it's been announced that I can't do that. Instead, I'll be wearin' one of them scarfs on my head to keep my hair from fallin' out into some stranger's bowl of chili and Barney'll have to wear one of them silly lookin' army hats that's made outta paper.

I thought for sure God wanted us to come to these mountains for a special reason—maybe to do somethin' special for Him. I never dreamed that I'd get stuck doin' somethin' I don't know one thing about and somethin' that's gonna take up all my time and energy. And Bernice, get a load of this. Barney and me will be workin' together six days a week —every day—day after day, side by side in the very same spot without a break from each other's company. Now tell the truth, Bernice. Could you and Hunter do that? Never in this world did I dream that me and Barney could.

Speakin' of dreamin, I keep havin' this same dream about the cafe business. In this dream, all these strangers are comin' in to eat and I don't know 'em from Adam, and they expect me to know how they like their eggs cooked, if they like onion on their burgers, if they want me to hold the mayo, and if they like their coffee black, and I'm supposed to smile at 'em when I feel like cryin' and when I wake up I'm so happy to know it's a dream but every time I go back to sleep I get a rerun of the same dream! Do you think it'll be this way in real life? If it is, I'll be nuttier than a fruit cake before long.

Barney don't have much to say about all this but he don't talk a lot. I'd give a pretty if he'd cut loose and run his mouth just one time. He's forced me to learn to read his mind. He thinks I can't, but I can. Anyways, he's cool as a cucumber and has made the cutest tables for the cafe. He stained 'em and put on that shiny stuff to protect 'em from cigarette burns and all. We put paneling on the walls, and I made yellow ruffled curtains to hang over the windows to match the yellow floor tile. It looks pretty and homey, Bernice. Barney said that he wants it to be a place where people will feel at home and know that we 'preciate 'em.

We decided to name our business "Barney's Place." That was my second choice. The first one bein' " Myrtle and Barney Bridges' Little Place In The Country." Barney said that my choice had too many words in it to get on a sign and I guess he's right. He usually is.

We open for business soon so set your alarm clock for 6:30 A.M. on Monday, October 11 because I need you to start prayin' for me precisely at 6:30. Whatever you do, Bernice, don't forget. This request is of vital importance. I just know —in my heart—that I need your prayers. In fact, call the prayer chairman of the W.M.U. at church and get my name in the prayer chain. I'll let you know when they can let up on the prayin'.

I have to close for now and get some sleep. Lord, I hope I don't dream tonight. Remember, we're friends forever.

Love,
Myrtle

First Day on the Job

My dearest Mama,

At the present time, I'm sittin' at a table in the cafe. We have finally put the Closed sign in the window. I told Barney that I wanted to write a letter. I failed to tell him that I sat down and can't get up! He's back in the kitchen singin' "Oh, Happy Day". I don't know how he can muster up enough energy to sing or has the spirit to even try.

Mama, there's people in the hospital that feel much better than I do. My feet feel like I've walked on hot coals without my shoes. And my legs feel like coffee's perkin' through the veins. Labor pains was nothin' compared to the way my back feels now. And get this, Mama. All this sufferin' for $19.00! I'm not talkin' about my tips, Mama. $19.00 is all we took in today.

Yes, ma'am, that's all we took in from 6:30 A.M. till 6:00 P.M. I can't go on. Life is not worth livin' under these conditions. No, Mama, I'm not gonna kill myself. It's gonna happen naturally if I have to do this work everyday.

Some people were cut out to work in the food business and some were not. I am in the latter group. Wonder why God didn't check this out better before He brought us up to these mountains?

One thing's for sure. I won't be able to serve Him and food at the same time. That won't be humanly possible.

Don't worry about me. If I die soon, you can rest assured that I was ready and willin' to go.

God's will be done. I love you.

Your daughter,
Myrtle

P.S. Everybody ought to be in the food business for at least one day. It'd make 'em 'preciate every bite they put in their mouth and the people that serve it to 'em.

Broken Promise

Dear Yvonne,

I don't know how to tell you this, honey, but your mama lied to you. I'm just gonna come right out and tell it like it is. I can't be with you when the baby's born, and I can't be there to help you after you come home from the hospital either. I know I'm lettin' you down.

As far as I know, I've never done that before and I don't want to now but I don't have a choice. We can't shut the door and walk off leavin' a business that's just got opened and expect to come back and start over again. And I can't come and leave your Dad here workin' on his own. That wouldn't be fair to him. I'd never have promised I'd be there if I knew how things was gonna be.

I really don't expect you to understand but do ask you to forgive me for breakin' my promise to you. As soon as you read this letter, I want you to pick up the phone and call Bernice and ask her if you can come over to visit for a spell. She promised to be there for you in my stead and I know she will be.

My heart is heavy and feels like it's bein' pulled in all directions. I must close now and try to get some sleep. Tomorrow will be here before I know it. Seems like the days are flyin' by. Your Dad's fine and sends his love.

Love,
Mama

Job Security

Dear Mr. Higgins,
 Betcha can't guess who this letter's from. It's me—Myrtle Bridges. I used to work for you.
 On my last day on the job, before I moved back to North Carolina, you told me to "keep in touch" and that I could have my job back if I ever wanted it because you said that I was a hard workin' lady and honest as the day is long. You *do* remember sayin' that, don't you?
 Mr. Higgins, I might be needin' that job again. You thought that I worked real hard for you, and shoot, I thought I did too, but to tell the truth, if I still had some of the pay left that you paid me over the years, I'd send it back to you. Mr. Higgins, I was grossly overpaid!
 Since Barney and me opened our cafe, I have never worked so hard in all my life. You wouldn't believe the hours we put in and the profit we don't make.
 But we don't have the problems you had with employees 'cause we can't afford any. You might say that Barney sleeps with the waitress, cashier, dishwasher and sweeper, and you know he's an honorable Southern gentleman so all them people's me!
 Barney's the cook and does all the orderin' plus he helps me wash dishes — that is, if he's not sittin' out front talkin' to the customers. He's the public relations person, at least, that's what he tells me. He must be a good un 'cause them people's smilin' when they come in and when they leave too. There's just not enough of 'em.
 Now, gettin' back to the reason for my letter. We've borrowed money on Barney's life insurance policy and hope and pray that it'll be enough to keep the doors opened 'til business picks up. If it's not, we might be hotfootin' it back to Florida, in which case, I'll be seein' you.

Your faithful ex-employee,
Myrtle Bridges

A Full Moon

Dear B.J.,

You're not gonna believe this but I'm gonna tell you anyways. Your dad and me drove into town last night to get a change of scenery and boy, did we ever get one!

I'm just about too embarrassed to tell you what happened but I'll try bein's I'm writin' about it and not lookin' you eyeball to eyeball.

I can feel my face gettin' red just thinkin' about it, but here goes. We was cruisin' along mindin' our own business and listenin' to the country station on the radio when a car passed us right fast like and then slowed down when it got around us. Three boys was in the car—two up front and one in the back seat, and they looked to be about eighteen years old. I believe they was students 'cause they had college bumper stickers on the car, and we was very near the campus. Well, anyways, to our surprise, the young man in the back seat proceeded to get up on the seat and I don't know how to say this—he dropped his drawers and how do you say it? He mooned your mama and dad right there in full view for all the world to see!

As soon as I realized what that boy was doin', I laid my head in my lap and screamed for your dad to shut his eyes. We're not in the habit of ridin' around starin' at people's rear ends, that's for sure.

"I can't shut my eyes, Myrtle," your dad said, "I'll run off the road."

"Don't look, Barney. Pretend you don't see him," I hollered. "That boy is no doubt homesick and missin' his mama so much that he's outta his head. I feel so sorry for him and his mama I could cry."

"I don't think he's out of his head but he shore is out of his drawers," your dad replied. In fact, he thought it was comical that we got mooned.

If I knew that boy's mama, I'd call her and tell her to quit worryin' 'bout him 'cause from the looks of his hiney, he ain't missed any meals since he got here.

I love young people but if I had my druthers, they'd refrain from doin' such a disrespectful thing. You wouldn't do such a thing, would you, B.J.?

Remember this, B.J., if you get real homesick to see your mama, for goodness sakes don't do anything that would embarrass our family. Just pick up the phone and call me collect. That makes more sense than doin' somethin' of such a wild nature as moonin'. The moon belongs in the sky where God put it. Not in the back seat of a car.

I love you and you had better behave like the gentleman I taught you to be.

Much love,
Mama

Coffee Can Friends

Dear Bernice,

Tell the W.M.U. members to keep up the good work and keep on prayin' for me. It's too soon to let up just yet. I'll let you know when they can ease off and devote their prayers to somebody else with more problems than me.

One of my problems has been settled though. But let me just start at the beginnin' and bring you up to date on what I've been goin' through.

Do you remember me sayin' in one of my many letters to you that a family from China had moved into our community and that I had added Yvonne's rice dish to our menu so's I have somethin' special to serve 'em when they come in to eat at " Barney's Place"? Well, they won't be comin' in 'cause they don't exist!

This tidbit of information was passed on to me last Friday in a unexpected way.

I was hummin' "Jesus Loves the Little Children" and was happy as a lark and for some reason I thought of the Chinese family. I've been so anxious to meet 'em but hadn't laid eyes on 'em as yet. Well, anyways, I asked a group of my mornin' coffee drinkers if they'd met the new people from China?

"What new people, Myrtle?" one of the men asked. "I don't know of any new people movin' in —much less people from China. Where'd you get such a notion?"

"Ya'll have been talkin' about them outsiders ever since we opened up 'Barney's Place' and I figured they was from China or somewhere like that," I said.

Well, I never seen such leg slappin' and laughin' in all my life. I was the only one in the room that didn't understand the humor in my comment.

Bernice, do you realize that you and Hunter was the only people we knew in Florida that wasn't outsiders?

My mountains friends informed me that if you wasn't born in this end of the county, then you're an outsider. Can you believe that? What difference does it make where you was born? The only thing of importance is makin' the place you're in a little better for the people there. And that's what I thought me and Barney had been doin' here. Givin' these sweet people a place to come and meet and eat.

Well, I lost my cool when I learned I was one of them "O" words and I gave them fellers a piece of my mind.

I said, "Do you mean to sit there sippin' on the coffee I made for you while I was still half asleep in a cup that I washed and carried to you like a servant and tell me I'm not kinda like family? I worry if you're not clean platers, fearin' you're comin' down with somethin'. Shoot fire, I've worried more about you fellers than I did my own young'uns when they was little. You see that 'welcome' sign over there on the wall? It's for you. I bet you say, " Do you think the 'outsider' will pour us another cup of coffee?"

About that time Barney said, "Shush up, Myrtle. These people are payin' our light bill and them people over at Blue Ridge Electric are waitin' for it today. We may as well start packin' tonight. We'll have to move outta here in the dark."

That's the bad part. But listen to the good part.

A few days later, one of them fellers come in real early and he had a coffee can in his hand. He whopped that can down on the counter and said, "Myrtle, did I hear you say the other day that you needed coins to make change with?"

"I sure do. Why?" I asked.

"Here's a coffee can full of change but I've not counted it yet. Count it when you've got time and use it. You can pay me later. I trust you, Myrtle," he said.

Bernice, a lump sprung up in my throat and I wanted to hug him. Now, that man wouldn't trust just anybody with his money, would he? And certainly not one of them outsiders.

It's very early and I must get ready to meet the day that the Lord hath made. He knew what He was doin' when He brought us to these mountains. He really did.

Love,
Myrtle, your friend forever

He's a Good 'Un

Dear Hazel,

My sanity is danglin' by a thread. This job is drivin' me up a wall. I'd trade places with Barney but he's a better cook than I am. He's got it made. He can hide back in the kitchen and take his time fryin' them burgers while I have to go out there and face them hungry customers.

Nothin' unglues Barney! He just works along and sings as he goes. You'd think he was just piddlin' around the kitchen at home casually makin' us a sandwich or something.

One day the cafe was full and I went runnin' back to the kitchen like a wild woman to see if one of my many orders was ready to be served and what do you think he was doin'? I'll tell you what he was doin' 'cause you'd never guess in a million years. He was leanin' against the kitchen wall munchin' on a cheeseburger!

"My Lord, Barney! What are you doin'?" I asked.

"I'm havin' lunch. Would you care to join me?" he replied.

"Them people out there's half starved," I said. "How can you take time to eat, leavin' me out there to face the crowd that's watchin' me like a hawk and hopin' everytime I walk out there that I'm gonna have their order in my hand. They're perched on the edge of their seats right ready to pounce on me. Here, I'll watch them burgers fryin', you go out there and face 'em like a man," I said.

By the time I'd had my say, he had finished his lunch, flipped them burgers over and then started singin' "Teach Me To Pray."

"Why don't you ask Him to teach you to hurry?" I said. "You already know how to pray."

See what I mean, Hazel? It's gettin' to me. Sometimes I flat out ask the Lord if He's aware of what I'm goin' through. I'm not the calm person my Barney is. Do you reckon I get on his nerves too? If I do, he don't show it. He's a good 'un.

Why don't you drive up for a visit and bring mama so's we can all enjoy the beauty of the mountains together?

Love to all the family,
Myrtle

Labor Pains

Dear Hazel,

It's a boy! A precious baby boy, and I'm so happy I could shout from the top of the mountain, "I'm a grandma at last."

The labor pains was difficult however, lastin' from early mornin' till dark. At times, they was almost unbearable and especially durin' the lunch rush when I couldn't sit down. Yvonne breezed right through her labor pains, though. But then, she and her hubby had took them birthin' classes and learned how to hee hee and that made all the difference in the world.

Let me start at the beginnin' so's not to confuse you.

Yvonne called me just as I had requested to tell me that she and hubby was on the way to the hospital and that her labor pains was about three minutes apart.

The first thing I did after I hung up the phone was to pray for her. I never worried about myself when I was expectin' like I worried about Yvonne. Well, anyways, approximately five minutes after my "Amen", *my* labor pains started!

At first, I thought it was gas pains but as the day wore on, I knew better. Of course, it didn't help matters any with me havin' to work and stay on my feet all day.

Barney noticed that I looked kinda strange like and asked what was wrong. "I'm havin' labor pains, Barney." Well, you'd have thought I was a nut or somethin' from the way he laughed.

"You're not havin' labor pains, Myrtle, it's in your head," he said. But it wasn't in my head, Hazel. The pain was located real low in my back precisely where the labor pains was when I was havin' my babies and he burnt me up, too and I said,

"Tell me, Barney Bridges, have you ever had a baby?"

"No," he said, "but I fathered three."

"Well, let me tell you one thing, buddy boy." I said. "I was there when you fathered them three and I was there when them three was born and there's no comparison to the two situations. "

Barney musta felt bad about it 'cause he offered to fix me some tea but I reminded him that one does not drink or eat while experiencin' hard labor.

Even if it was allowed, I couldn't have accepted it because I couldn't halfway swallow. When I'm extremely nervous my throat might near closes up on me. This went on all day until the call came that the baby had been born in perfect condition and that Yvonne was just fine. My labor pains stopped approximately one second after I hung up the phone.

At which time, Barney said, "Myrtle, darlin', why don't you sit down and let me fix you a little somethin' to eat. You've not eat a bite all day."

I said, "That's sweet of you, Barney. I'll have a super burger— all the way— fries, a side order of coleslaw, a strawberry shake and a cup of coffee to go with my apple pie. And make it snappy, Grandpa, I'm hungry as a bear!"

I'd had my heart set on bein' with Yvonne when the baby was born but it wasn't meant to be. I couldn't be by her side but the Lord was and that's the most important thing of all.

I'll send you the baby's picture just as soon as I get some.

Love,
Myrtle

We Aim to Please

Dearest B.J. and Dil,

Thought I'd better write to let you know how things are goin' up here in the hills. Not too good.

Now I know why people use to have big families. It's cause they knew they'd need help with the work. I know you wish you lived closer so's you could help us in this business, don't you? Seems like all we do is work.

I keep askin' God how He expects me to serve Him when all I ever get done is servin' people. But they're the nicest people a body could serve, that's for sure.

To prove my point, let me tell you what happened the other day. It was lunch time and our place was full.

Your Dad was movin' them orders out like a pro but I couldn't keep up with him 'cause in between servin' the food to the customers, I was takin' the orders, cleanin' the tables, answerin' the phone for takeouts and baggin' them takeouts and last, but not least, I was runnin' the cash register!

A sweet old lady was waitin' to be served. I know she musta been at least eighty years old. Her white hair was pulled back into a little ball on the back of her head and she had the sweetest smile on her face I ever saw. I had gone into the kitchen and when I come back out into the dinin' room, there she was —busy as a bee—clearin' off a table and she come bringin' the dishes back to the kitchen!

"Have you got a spare apron?" she asked. She said that she couldn't just sit there watchin' me work so hard. She musta enjoyed clearin' tables so much that she commenced to carrying orders to the customers. I write their name on the order if I know it and if I don't know it, I write somethin' like "Man in red hat or man in blue shirt."

Anyways, she carried a big order to a man that had on a red hat but so did six other men and this man had not ordered the cheeseburger, bowl of chili and fries that he was munchin' on. He had ordered a grilled cheese with no mayo. But he was sittin' there munchin' away and looked happy as a lark and I didn't want to rock the boat so I didn't say a word. I just kept bringin' them orders out and tried to keep a eye on my helper, in case she got 'em mixed up again.

When the man was ready to pay, I said, "I'll just charge you for what you ordered—not for what you ate."

He grinned and shook his head and said," No way. You can't make a livin' here doin' that. I ate every bite of it and I'm glad I got the wrong order. It was great!"

See what I mean? Then, when the lady finished eatin', I didn't want to take her money 'cause she had worked so hard tryin' to help me.

"No, honey," she said, "that's why we're still here in this world—to help one another. Besides, I don't know when I've had so much fun." She had visited and laughed with all my customers the whole time.

I treat my customers like they was company or somethin'. I want 'em to feel like they're comin' to their sister's house to eat and it's sure bud hard to charge family for their food.

Maybe after we're in business a little longer I'll get used to chargin' for the food and can stop worryin' if they don't eat ever bite of it. I mean, if they don't eat it all, should they have to pay for it? I have trouble with this.

We're extra particular about the appearance of our orders too. For instance, if a customer was to order eggs over light and one of the yokes was to break, we wouldn't serve it to 'em. No sir. Barney would fry another one and one of us would eat the runny egg if we had time. If we didn't have time, the dog would get it. He don't need 'em either. He's gettin' fatter than a pig.

Speakin' of pigs, our BBQ is outta this world, even if I do say so myself.

You know I'm not the braggin' type, but I'm proud of the way our business is doin'. Just the other day a woman said to me, "It feels good to come in here and eat. I look forward to the visit as much as the good eatin'."

She was my day brightener. At least, it's good to know that we're appreciated 'round here.

One thing's for sure. We try hard to please everbody and we're picky 'bout the way our sandwiches look too. They must have a little of the lettuce showin' around the edges of the bun. That makes 'em more enticin'. And the secret of a good hot dog is to squeeze the mayo out of the slaw before it goes in the bun. If you don't, it makes for a sloppy dog and I hate 'em that way, don't you? And we take pains to chop the onion up real fine so the flavor can blend in better. I just love it when my customer orders a hot dog and wants extra onion 'cause your Dad puts mustard on the bun first and get this—then the onion so's it won't fall all over the place —then the hot dog and whatever they wanted on top whether it be slaw or chili or both or just relish. But then some people do order ketchup only.

Anyways, when they don't see the onion right off the bat, the first thing they say is, "You forgot the onion." It does my heart good to say,"No, no. It's there. You just can't see it." All these things take extra time but they make for a more satisfied customer which is the very one that's payin' our bills. People tell us that we worry too much about little things, but I think not.

Your Dad's fine only he's puttin' in too many hours. We're workin' harder than we've ever worked before. We still love it here but I can't enjoy livin' in the Blue Ridge from the inside of a cafe!

Maybe after we get some help, we'll be able to see what mountain livin's all about.

Come up when you can for we'll not be gettin' away any time soon.

I love you both,
Mama

Grilled Cheese No Mayo

Dear Hazel,

I got your letter last week and fully intended to answer it before now but if you was here with me you'd know why you've not heard from me. Hazel, there's never a dull moment around this place.

In fact, it got down right excitin' back in the kitchen today. I had stuck orders plum across the grill for Barney to fix and had plainly marked one in red that said "Grilled Cheese-**NO MAYO**" I even underlined no mayo so's he'd see it and do it right.

Well, you'd thought that I had committed the unpardonable sin when I saw the mayo drippin' out of that sandwich and simply said, "Barney darlin', can't you read? That grilled cheese order had no mayo on it. I'm not about to carry it out to my customer. You'll have to make another one. Look, I even underlined NO MAYO. I can't hide back here in the kitchen doin' my thing like you can. I have to go out there and face my customers. And I can't sing while I do my work like you do, either. I'm too busy writin' down my orders to the customers specific request and tryin' to please 'em to the best of my ability and I'd 'preciate it if you'd do the same."

Well, Hazel, all of a sudden, Barney yanked that grilled cheese sandwich out of my hand and slung it across the kitchen and that thing splattered on the wall and commenced to slidin' down leavin' a trail of mayo and drippy cheese all the way to the floor!

I'd never seen Barney get that dramatic, and I didn't know what to say other than, "I hope that made you feel better, Barney, 'cause you've made one more mell of a hess. And another thing, in this world of starvin' people, it's a shame to waste perfectly good food." With that, I shot back out to the dinin' room and to the safety of my customers.

I'll tell you one thing. This place is gonna teach us patience— patience with customers and with each other.

Come up when you can. Wait till you taste our burgers. They're the best in town. But then, there ain't no other place out here to eat.

Give the family my love.
Myrtle

A Know-It-All

Dear Bernice,

Do you remember the dream I had before we opened "Barney's Place"? The one where I was worried about the customer's orders? Well, I'm happy to say that I do remember how customers like their burgers and coffee, too, for that matter. In fact, when I see one of our customers in town, I always think of the special way they order food.

For instance, in my mind I would say, "Oh, there's Mr. Hold The Onion Thompson with his Black Coffee Wife." Or there's John Extra Mayo Simpson. Food service is such a personal business. I've got one lady that comes up from Florida and when she's here, she always comes in for breakfast. Now, I know exactly how she likes her eggs cooked but I always ask her so's I can hear her say, "Over eva so lightly." You learn so much about the customer. You wouldn't believe just how much. I mean, a shoe salesman only gets to know what size shoe their customer wears and if their socks are clean, or how much they want to spend but I learn much much more about my people.

Did you know that some people want their coffee pipin' hot when they get it but they want a spoonful of ice dumped in it to cool it off right fast like before they start sippin' on it? One customer likes her hot dog with a shot of mustard all the way down the bun but, now get this, she wants half the hot dog covered with slaw and the other half covered with chili and then onion spread from end to end. When she orders her dog, I simply jot her name on the ticket and write "I'll fix it" since I already know exactly how she wants it. Besides, Barney won't take time to read my orders if they fill up the front side and continue on over on the back. I'm careful to keep the slaw and chili from mixin' too. She don't like 'em touchin'. I said all that to say this: I never dreamed I'd have the privilege of learnin' so much about people. This is a very interestin' business. I think I'm becomin' a real know-it-all in this community but in a good way, of course. And it feels good to be learnin' the likes and dislikes of my customers. I'm not sure, but I think me and Barney's startin' to fit in and that feels good too.

I got your card and was glad to know that you and Hunter are doing fine. How long will it be before ya'll can come up to see us? Do you miss me? I do you. Write soon.

Your friend forever,
Myrtle

The Gong Show

Dear Hazel,

It's been a spell since I wrote you but honey, I've been so busy. You'd understand if you was here with me.

Business keeps pickin' up and we're workin' steady all the time. I don't like to complain though. Lots of people don't have work. Some ain't able to work so I'm thankful we can.

I did tell Barney the other day that we needed to take time to stop and smell the roses. I do believe he'd druther keep workin' and smell the onions, so to speak.

He's got that super burger down pat. We ain't no McDonalds by no means, but his burger is gettin' to be well known in this end of the county.

We're gettin' use to bein' together all the time day and night. It ain't so bad. In fact, I can't think of anybody I'd druther be with than my Barney. He's got the best sense of humor and it rings out in that kitchen.

Let me tell you what he did the other day. I had asked one of my customers how he felt and he was in the middle of tellin' me the details of the operation he was gettin' over when one of my orders was ready to take to another customer.

I didn't notice the order was ready 'cause I was listenin' to my sick customer. I mean, if I ask how they are, I want to hear their answer. Don't you? Well, anyways, Barney needed to do something to get my attention so he took a fryin' pan and hit that thing with a big ladle and the racket bounced off the walls in the dinin' room like a ping pong ball. I was so embarrassed and excused myself and went runnin' back to the kitchen.

"That's not funny, Barney," I said. But it was and I couldn't keep a straight face to save my life when I seen him standin' there holdin' that big fryin' pan and just a grinnin' from ear to ear.

Hazel, it sounded like "The Gong Show" on television. If my sick customer had been havin' heart problems, he'd have probably died in my arms!

My friend Tweetsie offered to give us the bell that she and her hubby used to get each other's attention in their cafe now that they are closin' their business but Barney said we wouldn't last a week with that bell. Besides, he don't need one, does he?

I'd better go. Me and Barney's gonna go for a drive before it's too late to see the hills. I wish everbody could have the privilege of livin' in the mountains. Well, not everbody 'cause it'd be too crowded but I feel just a tad guilty when I look and see what the Lord hath made and think that some people will never get to see 'em.

But you come up anytime and see what I'm talkin' about.

Love,
Myrtle

Gentlemen, Start Them Engines

Dear Hazel,

You ain't gonna believe this but I'm gonna tell you anyways. I went with Barney to the Valleydale 500 Race in Bristol yesterday. I've never been a race fan exactly but that Barney does love it with a passion. Well, anyways, he said," Myrtle, would you like to go to the race with me this time?"

I answered, "Oh, Barney darlin', I would love to go, but you must remember that I don't know nothin' about racin'."

Just the fact that he asked me to go tickled me so good. I fixed us some fried chicken and egg salad sandwiches and off we went early Sunday mornin' like a couple of newlyweds.

Hazel, did you know that they park you smack dab in the middle of a cow pasture? I had a time keepin' up with Barney and out of the cow pies as we rushed to our seats. He practically run the whole way. I said, "Slow down for goodness sakes, Barney. We have reserved seats. They won't start the race 'til we get there." But would he listen to me? NO.

After we climbed what seemed like a mountain and finally got to our seats, my heart was poundin' like mad and my legs was weak as water. When I was able to speak, I told Barney that when the race started I wanted him to *whisper* to me what was going on so's we wouldn't disturb any of the people sittin' around us.

Hazel, have you ever heard them gentlemen start their engines? Ever pleasant sound and bird's song I ever heard passed right between my two ears and I couldn't hear a word Barney said to me and he was a screamin' at the top of his lungs! Now I know why they call it "Thunder Valley".

As soon as the race started, I knew I needed to start prayin' for them men in the cars. Hazel, they drove like wild men with nowheres to go except in a circle. Watchin' 'em made me a nervous wreck. Half the time I didn't watch. I had my eyes shut. I knew they couldn't shut their eyes to pray for safety so I did it for 'em. It bothered me a little but I even prayed for the boys in them beer sponsored cars. Just 'cause I don't indulge in the stuff, I still felt it my Christian duty to pray for them too. I 'specially liked that Coors feller 'cause he's got red hair and a Southern accent like my Barney. But my main concern was for Richard Petty. If anything was to happen to Richard I don't know what Barney would do. I knew that he'd be in no shape to drive home

and that there was 48,800 people at that race and I could just see it —
in my mind—me a tryin' to get our car out of that pasture with 48,798
other people all at the same time. So naturally, most of my prayin' was
for them two drivers.

Hazel, one prayer just led to another. I looked over to the
next section—the drinkin' section, mind you— and there was this
couple with marital problems. I could tell they was havin' marital
problems 'cause they wasn't sittin' nearly as close as me and Barney
was. We had snuggled up close together and held hands 'til Richard's
car had a close call and Barney got so excited that he squeezed so hard
he cut the circulation off in my hand. I kept my hands to myself after
that.

Anyways, as I was sayin', there sat this couple starin' straight
ahead. Ever once in a while he'd take a swig of that beer. He was
advertising for it too. He had on a shirt with a beer ad on the back and
a hat with a beer ad on the front! Don't that beat all? All of a sudden,
the girl reached over and took that beer can right outta his hand and
took a swig right there in front of all them people. Did not give it a
thought! One of the reasons they was havin' marital problems was
very obvious to me... She did not say "please" or "thank you." I wished
I had my copy of "Total Woman" with me. She needed to read it real
bad.

After I prayed for that couple with marital problems I looked
around at all the people there and it was a movin' experience for me.
You know what a people lover I am and I had never been with so many
people at one time!

Hazel, I looked across the track and could see thousands of
people, and I couldn't help but wonder about 'em and their problems
too. I felt it my Christian duty to pray for them too. Some of 'em
probably hadn't been prayed for in a long time.

You might wonder how I did this. It was easy as pie, Hazel. I
took Barney's binoculars and said, "Lord, I'm goin' to pray for the
section directly across the track in front of me. We'll call that section
A. Let's take it from the top. See that man in the bibbed overalls?
We'll start with him and go down to the bottom row to that boy in the
yellow shirt, all the way over to and includin' the pleasingly plump
lady, then back up to the top row to that hippie boy, then back over to
the man in the bibbed overalls." Then I said a prayer for all them
people in that section—section A. I then scooted around the track -in
my mind- and prayed for the people in section B and C. The people I
couldn't see, I handed over to God in one big pile along with the pit

crews and the people runnin' the concession stands. Now, I know God knew their problems 'cause He's even counted the hairs on their heads already, but I had to make sure I hadn't missed any of 'em. I couldn't bear the thought of it.

It didn't seem to bother anybody that I was lookin' away from the track half the time. Everbody else had their eyes glued to that track just a watchin' them cars go round and round and round— includin' Barney. He had plum forgot I was in the world. But once in a while I noticed him lookin' at some of them young girls with shorts on. I figured he was worried that they'd get a terrible sunburn. I was. Much more than half their bodies was exposed to the sun and to Barney.

Hazel, my attention went back to the track about then. A car come by that looked liked a box of Tide. I had missed it somehow when it hit the wall, but it was a sight to behold! I thought that car was goin' to fall apart right before my very eyes but "Bubbles" just kept a gettin' it and wouldn't give up. Whatta example he set for us. What if we handled our race in life that same way—never give up—keep on goin'. It was wonderful, Hazel.

Richard didn't win the race but at least he was safe and sound when the race ended, thanks to my prayers. The boy from Georgia won the race—the one with the red hair. I know in my heart that I had somethin' to do with it and it don't bother me one bit that he don't know this 'cause God knows and that's what counts.

You'll be glad to know that we got out of the cow pasture okay. The car was a mess but other than that everything was just fine. I may not go to another race. When you've seen one you've seen 'em all and besides, I enjoy talkin' to Barney too much, and he couldn't hear a word I said.

Thank goodness, God can hear us no matter what.

Love,
Myrtle

Got Any News?

Dear Bernice,

Your sweet little card with all them sixteen words arrived in the mail today. Don't get me wrong. I was happy to get it but, Bernice, honey, sixteen words!

What would be so hard about tellin' me what's goin' on in your life?

Have you been to the doctor lately?

Have you had your hair cut and colored again? Have you gained weight? Have you lost weight?

Have you got new neighbors? How's the weather?

Did your dog die?

Did your cat have kittens?

How are your young'uns? There has got to be some news in your life worth mentionin'.

Barney says that you've got news but think it's none of my business. I know better than that. Then, he went so far as to say, "She's workin' in her little greetin' card business at the flea market now. She's just too busy."

"She gave that up, Barney," I said. " She didn't want to work weekends."

He understood that till I told him that the flea market wasn't open but on them two days.

Then he said, "She's busy with her grandchildren. She's got six, ain't she, just like us?"

"Yea, and they live 2,000 miles away from her," I told him. "Got anymore excuses you want to dish out for her?"

Mercy, Bernice, when we lived near each other we was closer than sisters. The only difference was you didn't have to do any writin'. We either talked face to face or on the phone.

The arthritis in my neck come from holdin' the phone on my shoulder while I ironed and talked to you at the same time.

Remember how we could cook a meal without hangin' up? That was before cordless phones. Our cords stretched so far we coulda used 'em for clotheslines.

Remember the time I said I had to stop talkin' and make some meatballs? You said, "How do you make 'em, Myrtle? I've never made any."

We made a pot of meatballs together as we talked. I bet you remember that 'cause Hunter was tryin' to call you to tell you his truck had broke down and the line was busy for a long time. He was slightly upset when he finally got through to you, but he got over it when he tasted them meatballs, now didn't he?

Anyways, like I told Barney, I like to write. You don't. You like to sew. I don't.

"You don't have to tell me that, Myrtle. I know it," he said.

Bernice, why should I buy material and a pattern, cut it out and let it sit on the machine until it's out of style? Besides, that sewin' machine ain't been plugged in since 1978! If Barney wants me to be a fashion designer, we'll have to get outta the hardware business. There's just so much a woman can do- even a woman in this day and time. Don't you agree?

He said he wasn't wantin' me to be a fashion designer. He was thinkin' more along the line of sewin' on buttons!

Now when you get this letter don't think you've got to answer right back like I did. I know that bothers you to send a card and get a reply by return mail. Take your time and wait at least a week or so and then answer. And a card will be fine. I'll appreciate any news you might or might not have, honey.

The most important thing is to remember that we're friends forever. Okay?

Love,
Myrtle

P.S. My answers to the same questions I asked you are as follows: No, yes, yes, no, no, it's pourin' the rain, don't have one, ditto, fine!!

Room With Two Views

Dear Bernice,

Got your letter today and might near cried when I read it. I know exactly how you feel about the way Hunter works so hard.

You asked me how you could make him slow down before it's too late. If I knew the answer to that question, I wouldn't be married to a workaholic!

Barney's like Hunter for the world. He works all the time and it's tellin' on him too. I get so frustrated with him sometimes I feel like boppin' his jaws. Of course, I wouldn't lay a hand on him no more than he'd harm me, bless his heart.

As a matter of fact, let me tell you precisely how important his work is to him.

Last week his old ulcer started actin' up just a tad and I said, "Barney, darlin' don't you think you should go to the doctor before your bellyache kicks into high gear?"

"No," he said, "it'll settle down before long. Don't worry about me."

Well, it didn't settle down and the pain got worse and worse. He couldn't eat or sleep. So as we was gettin' ready for work one mornin', I said, "Let's don't open up today, Barney. Let's go to the doctor this mornin' and have that ulcer seen after."

"No, no, Myrtle," he argued, "we'll close early after the lunch rush and I'll go then."

Well, Bernice, by the time he left for the doctor's office he was hurtin' somethin' awful and get this, wouldn't let me go with him. Said there was no need for me to tag along. So I stayed home and he struck out in the car by his lonesome. Two hours later he called soundin' kinda pitiful like.

I said, "What's wrong, Barney darlin'? What did the doctor say?"

"You'll have to get somebody to haul you over here to get the car," he moaned.

"What's wrong with the car?" I yelled.

"Nothin's wrong with the car, Myrtle, " he answered, "but the doctor's put me in the hospital, so bring me my pj's and bathrobe."

Bernice, I was already poutin' 'cause he wouldn't let me go with him to the doctor, and when I had to hitch a ride to the hospital, I was fumin' and was so mad I could of eat nails. There ain't nothin' wrong with my stomach.

Anyways, I had planned to give him a piece of my mind for bein' so stubborn, but when I rushed into the hospital room and seen him all tucked in that bed wearin' that little gown I felt so sorry for him I couldn't stand it.

All's I could do was sit there and hold his hand, but every once in a while I'd kiss it. It no longer mattered that he was a workaholic—nothin' mattered. I just wanted him back so's he could work or do whatever he wanted to do.

He tried to say somethin' to me but I wouldn't let him speak.

"Don't talk, Barney," I whispered. "Save your energy."

Besides, I was afraid that he thought he was gonna die and wanted to tell me how much he loved me while he could. This might near broke my heart and I wouldn't let him speak.

But he snapped at me, Bernice, and said, "Myrtle, I've got to tell you somethin' whether you want to hear it or not. I've got to go to the bathroom so let go of my hand and move out of the way."

"Well, excuuuuse me. Why didn't you say so, Barney?" I asked.

Bernice, when he headed for the bathroom, it hit me like a bolt outta the blue. I had plum forgot to bring his bathrobe. And I think I forgot to write and tell you about the time me and Barney got mooned. I'll do that later.

I cannot believe that they expect decent God fearin' people to wear them dinky hospital gowns that won't stay tied in the back.

I said, "Barney Bridges, you stay in that bathroom till I run over to K-Mart and buy a bathrobe." I flew outta that hospital, down the steps to the parkin' lot, into the car and to K-Mart quicker than it's took you to read this letter so far.

I parked in a space marked for the handicapped since I was on one of them emergency medical errands and proceeded to rush to the men's department. Luck was with me 'cause that blue light was flashin' like a beacon in the night. It was lovely. I grabbed a one-size-fits-all robe and scurried up front to the check out which had a long string of customers waitin' their turn.

I did somethin' I've never done before, Bernice. I marched right up to the man standin' at the head of the line and said, "Excuse me, sir. Could I step ahead of you, please? I'm in a hurry to get this robe to my husband. He's over in the hospital right now wearin' one of them backless gowns. Do you mind?"

"Go right ahead. I don't mind at all. I can relate to that," he said, as he stepped aside.

He was so nice. In fact, someone else standin' in line shouted out, "Hurry."

I did hurry. But by the time I got back to Barney's room he was already in bed. One of them nurses had helped him back from the bathroom.

Bernice, have you took a gander at any nurses lately? They're younger and prettier than they was the last time I was in the hospital.

Thank goodness, Barney wasn't there for long, and now he's back to work and happy as can be.

Come to think of it, we should be thankful for our faithful, hard-workin' husbands rather than gripin' about 'em.

I hope this letter has helped you to feel better 'bout things. I've been away a long time but remember, I'm only a thought away and we're friends forever.

Love,
Myrtle

The Gatherin'

Dear Bernice,

You shoulda been here last week. Yvonne and Camille come up for a visit, and I got this bright idea to do somethin' special so they could get to know some of my new friends.

Well, one of my friends, Peggy Sue, had just started sellin' Tupperware and needed to book a party so I told her I'd have one. You know how I love to entertain and all. That way, I figured I could kill two birds with one stone, so to speak. I wish I hadn't used that expression. I love birds.

Anyways, the evenin' was a "learnin' experience" for us all. In the first place, I could tell that Yvonne and Camille was just a tad jealous of Lizbeth. She's the young girl that helps me in the cafe. I love her like she was my own young 'un, and when they get to know her, they'll love her too.

Anyways, just as Peggy Sue had introduced herself and started on her sales pitch, the phone rang. It was Leonard, Lizbeth's husband, sayin' he needed to talk to her real bad. I didn't want to interrupt Peggy Sue, so I eased over and whispered to Lizbeth that the call was for her. When she got up, she accidently knocked over one of Peggy Sue's displays, but Peggy Sue was very gracious and didn't let on like it bothered her at all.

We knew somethin' was wrong when Lizbeth slammed the phone down and said, "He knows better than to call me that."

"Call you what, Lizbeth, darlin'?" I asked. My girls looked at me as if to say, "Lizbeth what?"

Everbody perked right up and waited to hear her answer though, cause she had tears the size of peas running down her face.

"Heifer, that's what," she moaned. "He loves to call me his 'little heifer' and I can't stand it."

"Mercy, I thought it was gonna be somethin' terrible for goodness sakes," I said. "Barney's pet name for me is worse than that. Don't cry, honey."

"What's Barney's pet name for you, Myrtle?" Lizbeth asked.

About that time, Peggy Sue said, "Myrtle, do you mind? I'm tryin' to make a livin' here, and I don't have all night. Can I please get on with my demo?"

"Of course, you can, Peggy Sue," I answered, but went on to say, "Lizbeth, right after my surgery, before we come to the mountains,

Barney commenced to callin' me "BB." He spoilt me while I was recoverin', and I thought he was usin' the initials for "Barney's Baby". Well, I found out that wasn't it at all.

One day, I just come out and asked him what "BB" stood for and was flabbergasted when he said, "Bubble Belly."

It was down right uncomfortable for me to suck in my stomach after my surgery so I didn't even try. Now I try, and it's downright impossible.

Well, Bernice, even my own young 'uns laughed at that. In fact, everbody in the room laughed, with the exception of Peggy Sue. She just stood there admirin' her set of tumblers.

"Laugh if you want to," I said. "Maybe ya'll should take a break and stand up and look down at your toes. Evidently, some of ya'll ain't tried to do that lately."

Right about then, I noticed Ernestine was lookin' strange like and she said," You'd never guess what Kermit calls me, and I wouldn't tell you for all the money in Hound Ears."

"You mean it's worse than 'Bubble Belly'?" I asked.

"Much worse," she replied.

I said, "On a scale of one to ten for worseness how bad is it?"

"It's a nine, at least," she shot back.

Next thing I know, Claudine piped up and said, "You're among friends, Ernestine. You can tell us."

Claudine's such a sweet, gentle person, and she promised Ernestine that we wouldn't laugh if she told us Kermit's name for her. We all swore on our friendship that we wouldn't laugh, but precisely when Ernestine blurted out that name, I took a swig of my orange sherbet punch.

Bernice, I got strangled and sprayed that punch all over Claudine's new sweat shirt. The one that has "Give Peace A Chance" sprawled all across the front.

Well, anyways, I went into one of my laughin' fits. The kind my girls call "Crafhin". It's a wild combination of cryin' and laughin' at the same time. Remember? You've seen me do it before.

Ernestine jumped up and run to the bathroom with Claudine right on her heels sayin' "Myrtle didn't mean to laugh, honey. I know in my heart she didn't do it on purpose. She ain't like that." Only Claudine don't say ain't. I said that.

Peggy Sue was practically hollerin' and said, "Ladies, have you placed your orders yet? Would you like to book a party?"

It was evident that Ernestine had more on her mind than partyin' right then. It mighta been the place to ask such a question, but it sure wasn't the time.

Bernice, I was so upset 'cause I had laughed and hurt Ernestine's feelin's that I snapped at her and said, "Peggy Sue, why don't you just take your Tupperware and— pack it?"

I couldn't believe my ears. Poor Peggy Sue, I wouldn't hurt her feelin's for nothin'.

"What in the world has got into you, Mama?" Yvonne screamed.

"She ain't the same, is she, Yvonne? She's changed. It must be that spring water she's been drinkin'. I bet she's havin' chlorine withdrawal," Camille yelled. She can get very emotional at times. She's like her dad for the world.

When I finally got control of myself, I looked at Lizbeth and noticed that she had mascara runnin' down her face. "Lizbeth, honey. You've got mascara all over your face," I said.

"You can't talk, Myrtle. You've got orange sherbet up your nose!" she promptly replied.

I run to the bathroom to blow my nose but Ernestine wouldn't open the door.

"Go join the party, Myrtle," Claudine said, when she stuck her head out the door. She's a lot stronger than I had give her credit for. She held Ernestine back and reached for a tissue and said, "Here, Myrtle. You need to use this."

Finally, she talked Ernestine out of the bathroom, and the two of them set down next to me with Claudine in the middle, of course.

There she sat, lookin' so peaceful like she had everything under control, but her shirt was soakin' wet.

Bless her heart, she had tried to wash out the sherbet while she was in the bathroom with Ernestine but it wouldn't come out. I noticed then that she had some on her "Save the Dolphin" headband too.

"I bet she tells Barney my nickname before she goes to bed tonight," Ernestine wailed, as she pointed them long fingernails at me.

"Sure, Ernestine," I said, as I tried to lean around Claudine. "I'm gonna put it up on the bulletin board in the cafe too, for all the world to see. You know good and well I won't tell Barney. I don't tell your dad everything. Do I, girls?"

"Well, you can sure bud tell him this," Peggy Sue yelled. "I have never, in all my born days been a witness to such a gatherin' as this. You've all been poppin' up like bread in a toaster all night. One minute somebody's laughin'. The next minute somebody's cryin', and you've not stopped runnin' your mouths since I got here. Now, listen up. I'm not askin' this question again. Are ya'll gonna give me any orders or not?"

"Of course, we are, Peggy Sue," I said. "Write me up a set of them tumblers. I can give 'em as a shower gift. No matter what the color scheme is, at least one of them jobbies will blend right in."

The girls are back in Florida now, so call 'em when you have a chance. They'll probably tell you 'bout their trip here. They both enjoyed meetin' my friends.

I bet you wonder what Ernestine's nickname is, don't you? If you won't tell Hunter, I'll give you a hint. I promised Ernestine I wouldn't broadcast it, but I'd trust you with my life. Here's the hint: I went to town yesterday to buy a *Satchel Butt* I couldn't find one. Did you get it? If you didn't, read it again. I went to town yesterday to buy a *Satchel Butt* I couldn't find one. Makes "Bubble Belly" sound plum delightful, don't you think?

Well, I gotta go. Remember, we're friends forever.

Love,
Myrtle

And Then There Was curls

Dear Bernice,

I wish you was here gazin' on what I'm lookin' at. I've never seen such perfect gorgeous little curls in all my life. You know how, when you first get a permanent, the curls are kinky and won't dangle the way you want 'em to. Well, that's not the case with this perm's curls. I only wish they was on my head instead of Barney's. I try not to covet, but in this case, I can't help myself.

I hadn't mentioned to you that he was gettin' a perm 'cause I didn't want to worry you with my problems. However, worse did come to worse and I'm married to a completely different lookin' man, and you know that I was perfectly satisfied with the man I had.

It's a long story, but one that needs to be told, so sit down, prop your feet up and read on.

Barney got it in his head that he was gettin' a perm. He had one of the young girls here pick him up a home perm in town, which was fine with me 'cause you know what one of them jobbies go for in a beauty parlor. Anyways, he said that I could go with him to her house so's she could put the perm in. I might mention that she's got blonde hair and blue eyes the size of robin eggs.

I told him, "I'm here to tell you I'm goin' with you, Barney. The last time some sweet young thing run her fingers through your hair it was me and I intend to be as close to you as your skin when it happens again."

Well, we got there and the girl's mama said, "Trixie will work on him in the kitchen. Do you want to sit in there and watch?"

I really did want to watch but didn't have the nerve so I flat out lied and said, "No, I sure don't."

I was a nervous wreck and so was the girl's mama. She said that she knew what I must be goin' through and took my hand and squeezed it.

"Could this be a mid-life crisis?" she asked.

"I don't know, but if he's jokin' and don't go through with it, Trixie can keep the perm for her trouble," I replied. Bernice, I thought he was jokin'. But he was as serious as a heart attack.

As we was sittin' in the den havin' silent prayer, the fumes from that perm commenced to driftin' in on us, and Trixie's mama had to open the front door so's we could breathe easier.

She sat down on the couch beside me and squeezed my hand again and said, "It's happenin." I couldn't have got through it without her, bless her heart.

We could hear Barney coughin' and beggin' for a towel to bury his face in. I pictured his head covered in them pink rollers and him a gaspin' for air and I got so tickled I thought I'd fall off that couch.

Bernice, we both busted out laughin' at the same time and got downright slap happy. Barney didn't hear us though 'cause he was makin' so much racket coughin' his fool head off.

You know me and how I am. If I feel like laughin' I have to laugh. I can't hold back. Well, I learned how to hold back. When I took my first look at Barney's curls, all's I could think of was little Shirley Temple just a singin' "On the Good Ship Lollipop." But I didn't laugh out loud—just on the inside. You would have been proud of me, I know.

Barney thought that with a perm one does not have to worry at all with one's hair. I could of told him different but some things are best left unsaid. By mornin', them curls had got lots more spring in 'em and Barney was frantically huntin' him a hat to wear before we opened up the cafe.

Customers even offered me a dollar to yank that hat off so's they could see his hair better. But I said, "No way, Jose."

Everything was okay 'til that perm started interferin' with our love life. I had got ready for bed one night and had put on a new nightie. Barney hadn't laid eyes on it as yet so I was anxious to see his face when he saw me wearin' it. I thought he was ready for bed too 'cause he'd been in the bathroom quite a while. When he didn't come out I got worried and knocked on the door to check on him. Bernice, when he opened that door he was standin' there in his "Fruit of the Looms" with a hot towel wound around his head givin' his self one of them hot oil treatments!

I lost my cool, Bernice. I said, "Barney Bridges, you've spent more time and money on them curls of yours than I've spent on my hair in four years. Looky there, you've got conditioner, protein, a oil kit, shampoo for curly hair, one for permed hair and one for hard-to-manage hair. You've got a hair pick and two kinds of wide-tooth combs. If there's anything around here that could use a little hot oil treatment, it's my back!" With that, I slammed the door of his beauty parlor and went to bed. Of course, I didn't stay mad for long. Barney's got a way 'bout him. He's so dadburn easy goin'. I wouldn't trade him for the world.

Bernice, I think I'll sign off and call Trixie. I'm gonna see if she'll put me in a perm tomorrow. If my prayer is answered, I'll strut out of that kitchen with my hair lookin' ever bit as good as Barney's.

Love, Myrtle
Your friend forever

Pony Express

Hello Bernice,

Well, I waited for the mailman to get here before I started this letter. I felt sure one of your dinky post cards would arrive in today's mail. But did it? No. Did Florida pass a law to stop outgoin' mail? I think not.

Please read over the statements listed below and circle the appropriate letter.

a- Our mama cat died and I'm havin' to feed five kittens around the clock.

b- I've been too busy with all my many friends to write.

c- I can't remember promises I make to friends.

d- I agree with the sayin' "Outta sight - outta mind".

e- Henry, our iguana, is sittin' on my pile of post cards and won't move.

f- A coconut dropped on my head and my vision is blurred.

g- I miss you just as much as you miss me and I will write soon.

Please return this letter as soon as possible. I remain your friend forever.

Myrtle

"10-4"

Dear Cora,

Thank you so much for the lovely card from Las Vegas, Nevada. My, my, how excitin' it must have been when you won $20.00. I asked Barney, "Wonder how much Cora spent to win $20.00?"

He said, "Don't ask her that, Myrtle. People only want to talk about what they won, not what they lost to win." Of course, I wouldn't ask you such a personal question. You know me, Cora. I'm not nosey. Wait, I take that back. I discovered, quite by accident, that I am just a tad nosey.

It all started when Barney announced that he wanted a scanner for the store. I pitched a fit and told him I didn't want one of them things in the store botherin' me. I do believe I called him nosey 'cause he wanted one.

Of course, it wasn't but a few days till he proceeded to hook one up, right in front of my nose, so to speak, directly in front of the cash register. Cora, I can't help but hear everthing that's goin' on. At first, I turned the volume on low so's I couldn't listen. But as time went on, I listened more and more. And now, the volume stays on high so's I won't miss nothin'.

Cora, did you know that one can speak nearly a full sentence and use very little of the alphabet? It's the beatinest thing I ever heard. Them people talk in numbers and it's common knowledge what they're sayin'. If your answer is "yes" to my question, you could of said "10-4". See what I mean? You know that commercial where you can hear a pin drop when "everybody listens"? Well, that's how it is in the store when the action starts on the scanner. If I'm handin' back change and the scanner comes on, my hand will stop in mid-air and I listen! Not just me, Cora, everbody listens. "What'd she say? Where's the fire? Who are they chasin'?" I might be nosey, Cora, but I ain't alone, believe me. Good comes from my "interest" (that sounds better) 'cause when I hear about people havin' trouble, I pray for 'em. Not meanin' to say that I say, "Let's have a word of prayer", I don't do that, but in my heart I do pray. I feel like if they need a ambulance, the police or firemen, somebody's needin' a prayer too, don't you think?. I'm serious, Cora. Think about it.

Mercy, I didn't mean to sound like a preacher. I just love to think of ways to be of help and that's one good way. Now, gettin' back to what I was sayin' about learnin' scanner talk and how one can save time with it. Just the other day, a man come runnin' in the store and said, "Do you know who owns the cows up around the curve?"

"I sure do," I answered. "Why?"

"They're in the road," he told me.

I didn't do a thing in this world, Cora, but pick up the phone and call my friend Gert. When she answered, I said, "Gert, this is Mert. We've got a 10-18 with a 10-68." She knew right off the bat that my call was urgent and there was livestock on the highway! She then made the call to round the cows up pronto! Don't that beat all? And to think that I'd never in this world had the chance to learn the numbers language if I'd stayed in the city.

Cora, will you and Homer be up to see us anytime soon? Hope you just said "10-4."

Let us hear from you before long.

Love,
Myrtle, your friend forever

All Choked Up

My dearest Bernice,

How in the world are you? Bein's you ain't heard from me in quite a spell, I thought I'd better check in and let you know that we're still alive and well.

However, last week, I come close to leavin' this world. Bernice, I ain't kiddin'.

Well, let me start at the beginnin' and you'll see how I almost became your late friend.

Me and Barney was at the store workin' when the phone rung. It was Cora. You remember meetin' her, don't you? She's married to Homer, Barney's best friend from high school days.

Anyways, as I was sayin', Cora called to say that they was in the mountains and was plannin' to drop by and spend the night. Now, that was fine with us 'cause we wanted to visit but since I didn't have time to cook on such short notice and wasn't home to do it anyways, Barney said, "Let's go to Shoney's."

So we headed to Shoney's after we closed the store. We had no sooner set down when our good friends Ernestine and Kermit come in and set down just in front of us. We introduced them to Cora and Homer and there we set like one big, happy family.

We'd finished eatin'- well, Barney hadn't. He was still eatin' that red Jell-O he loves so well, when my near-death-experience come in. Just as I took a big swig of my tea, Homer come up with one of his funny remarks and I got choked. Bernice, I mean really choked! The obituaries flashed in front of my very eyes and I was in 'em! That tea wouldn't go down and that tea wouldn't come up. All's it did was block out my air.

For what seemed like minutes, I tried to breathe but couldn't. Oh, how I wished my doctor friend, Levern, was with me.

"Can't these people see I'm dyin'?" I cried out, in my mind.

I answered my own question with, "No, they can't. They're too busy."

Barney was too busy eatin' that blamed red Jell-O and Homer was too busy runnin' his mouth. Cora was too busy puttin' on that fresh red lìpstick of hers.

"This is such a waste," I thought. "All's they'd have to do is hit me on the back and they could save my life and be a hero."

One of 'em finally said," Are you all right, Myrtle?"

"Thank God, praise be, I'll live," I thought, as I frantically shook my head side to side. But did they do anything? No!

I was fadin' fast when Cora blotted her lips and nonchalantly said, "Barney, I think Myrtle's chokin'." No, now that I think about it, she said, "Barney, Myrtle ain't breathin'. Her face is purple."

Barney sprung into action. He pulled his plate over away from me, switched his fork to his left hand, took another bite of that red Jell-O and with his right hand, he hit me on the back. Did not miss a bite!

I started coughin' my fool head off and finally cleared my windpipe out.

Ernestine turned around about then, just as wide-eyed as could be, and said, "People, don't you know when somebody's chokin'? Myrtle, can you breathe now?"

Ernestine can tell it like it is when she gets excited. Besides, we're best of friends and she didn't want to lose me.

Barney said, "We asked her if she was all right and she didn't say nothin'."

When I could finally talk, I said, "I was bruisin' my brain swingin' my head side to side. That should of told you somethin'. Shoot fire, eat your Jell-O," I snapped. "That's what you're gettin' for Christmas- a case of red Jell-O. I never knew it meant so much to you."

After the excitement was over, we settled down and had a good visit. Sure wish we could have a good visit too. Come up when you can.

Love, Myrtle
Your friend forever

A Bloomin' Bouquet

Dear Bernice,

I declare if you're not nervy to write and ask me to send you the story of how I got my name so's you can read it for entertainment at your next "Flower Lovers Club" meetin'. This will be the umpteenth time I've told it to you, but I'll tell it one more time and in precisely the same way it was told to me by my grandma.

Just before my mama was born, my grandma and grandpa was tryin' to decide on a name for her.

"What will we call our first baby, Sneed?" my grandma asked.

"Aster, my dearest," grandpa replied, "if we're fortunate enough to have a girl I'd like to name her, and she shall be named for a flower just as her mother was."

"Good, and if we have a son, I will name him. Perhaps, I'll give him a Bible name," grandma happily responded.

"Fine," grandpa said. "In fact, if we should be blest with other children later on you can name the boys, and I'll always name the girls."

Well, the first child was a girl and grandpa named her Dahlia. Before long, grandma discovered that she was expectin' again and began to familiarize herself with boy names. A lot of good it did her because grandpa got to name their second child Hyacinth.

Then, along came Rose, followed by Fern. (Grandpa wanted to name her Foliage but grandma pitched such a fit that he had to settle for Fern).

Grandpa was the proudest papa around but one thing bothered him somethin' awful. That bein' that grandma hadn't been privileged to name one single child as yet. That just didn't seem fair to him so they decided to have another baby so's grandma could have one more shot at it.

Well, she missed her shot and grandpa named baby number five Lily.

The little girls was precious and was always the center of attention at church.

But one Sunday in particular, grandpa's temper flared just a tad when he overheard his darlin' little girls bein' referred to as "The Floral Arrangement!" Grandma was afraid that he was gettin' too riled up so she sweetly reminded him that the baby namin' was his idea in the first place.

"I realize that," he snapped, "but I wasn't expectin' A Bloomin' Bouquet!" After he had cooled down, he surprised grandma with this statement.

"Aster, darlin'," he pleaded," what do you say if we have one more baby and you just concentrate on a boy's name. I'm not goin' to give it a thought and surely you'll get to name young'un number six."

That's what grandma did, too. It was easy as pie for her 'cause she'd been patiently waitin' to use the name she'd chose since before Dahlia, my mama, was born. But little baby Moses turned out to be Mimosa!

My grandpa really had determination and tried to give grandma one last chance at namin' a baby. But you know what? When little Coral-Bell was born, he was just as happy with her as he was when Dahlia, Hyacinth, Rose, Fern, Lily and Mimosa was born.

A few years later, I was born, and I know that grandpa musta been secretly hopin' for a grandson. However, I'm proud to say that he asked to name me and my mama and daddy agreed, only they refused to call me by my full name—which is Crepe Myrtle.

So, there's the story just as it was told to me years ago by my precious grandma, Aster Morgan. I hope your club members enjoy hearin' it. I wish I was there so's I could tell it to 'em in person but I can't be. Instead, I'll be there in spirit, and remember we're friends forever.

Love, Myrtle

Hee Haw

Dear Hazel,

It's been a while since I had the privilege of gettin' a letter from you. How's things goin' in your neck of the woods?

All's well here. This is a lovely time to be in the mountains because of the color and all. Mama and Sissy was here not long ago and we had the nicest visit. They wanted to be here when the leaves was changin' color.

We went ridin' around one afternoon and I drove 'em over to Ashe County so's they could enjoy the beauty there.

While we was out, I suggested that we do a little shoppin' so we went to this shop in Mountain City.

Sissy spotted some bibbed overalls and said, "Myrtle, do you ever wear these things?"

"Lord have mercy, no!" I answered.

"Why not?" she asked. "I think they're darlin'. Let's try some on."

"No, there's too many people in here. I don't want to be seen wearin' 'em."

"They'll look good on us. We're not over the hill yet, Myrtle," Sissy said.

Well, we each took a pair in the dressin' room and I could hear her as she struggled to pull hers up. I felt a little sorry for her 'cause I wasn't havin' any trouble at all with mine. In fact, I had room left to spare.

"Do yours fit, Myrtle?" she called out.

"Actually, precious, they're a little big on me." I hated to tell her that but what could I say?

"What did you say? I don't believe it." Then, she about broke her neck gettin' out to see what I looked like wearin' 'em.

She looked like she had been melted and poured into hers.

"Are these things suppose to be snug? Look at how baggy they are on me," I said.

"Something's wrong here," Sissy said. Let me see that size."

The overalls was the same size but was made of different material and cut bigger.

"I ain't skinnier than you are, Sissy, I'm sorry to say. It's the way my overalls are made."

"Well, I certainly hope that's what it is. Let me try 'em on."

Now, Mama was sittin' right there listenin' to us and I'm sure was just a prayin' that we'd have more sense than to buy bibbed overalls.

"Mama, if we was to buy these, would you be caught out in public with us wearin' 'em?" I asked.

"Of course. But, I'd stay put in the car," she answered.

We left the overalls behind and on the way home, me and Sissy talked about days gone by when we worried about bein' thin!! Don't that beat all?

I really do like them overalls on younger girls. Come to think of it, I might go back and buy a pair to wear in the privacy of my own home but it'd have to be when Barney wasn't there. I don't think he'd appreciate that style on me.

I can hear him, in my mind, "Good grief, Myrtle. What was you thinkin' when you bought them things?"

Oh well, I can dream, can't I? Do come up to see us, Hazel. We'd love to have you.

Love, Myrtle,
your friend forever

That Day Has Come

Dear Cora,

It's been a while since I heard from you. Have you been on one of them trips to the Bahamas? Don't guess me and Barney'll ever take one of them trips 'cause from what I hear about 'em, they practically force feed you.

Well, they don't use force to make you eat but they set the temptation before you and it's hard to resist, ain't it?

Speakin' of food, it makes me think of this diet me and Barney was on a while back. It all started when he told me that he intended to lose weight and he showed me this diet a customer had give him.

"Barney, darlin'," I said, "We can go on this diet together. Won't that make it easier on you?"

"Whatever you want to do, Myrtle," he said. Bless his heart, he don't say much about my weight but he still calls me "Bubble Belly" ever once in a while. So I feel like he still remembers the skinny little thing I was when we got married. I could just kick myself when I think back to how I worried 'cause I was thin!! Can you imagine that?

My doctor said, "Myrtle, stop worrying about being thin. There'll come a day when you'll wish you was just like you are now."

That day has come, Cora. Anyways, like I was sayin', we went on this diet. You know, the one where you eat certain food for three days with nothin' in-between meals and no junk food at all.

It wasn't easy, but we stuck to it. By suppertime, we was half starved 'cause them five crackers and the dabble of cottage cheese we'd had for lunch was long forgot. Beets never tasted so good to me. Barney watched me like a hawk to make sure I had put the full 1/2 cup of carrots on his plate.

"Looks to me like you got more carrots on your plate than me."

"Barney, I do not. I can't believe you said that!" I told him.

He's not himself when he's starvin'. And you shoulda seen him eatin' his apple one night. I'll admit that apple was outta this world, but he ate all but the stem and the seeds! I tried to give him half of mine, well, not half, but maybe a quarter of it, but he wouldn't accept it 'cause that woulda upset the chemical balance and messed up the diet. He's got the will power.

He fixed our ice cream one night and I knew it didn't look like a cup. (One night we could have one full cup.)

"Barney, are you sure this is a cup of ice cream?" I asked. I had already looked to see how much we was allowed and was lookin' forward to one full cup.

"It's half a cup," he told me. "Can we have a full cup tonight?" he asked.

"We sure can," I happily announced.

He jumped outta that chair like he had won the lottery to get more ice cream. Bless his heart, that was the best news he'd had all day.

Laughter is as good for the soul and body as a healthy diet, don't you think? We laughed quite a bit and lost some weight.

But thinkin' back to other diets, the best "diet" laugh Barney ever gave me was when we was on one that let us eat only bananas and drink skimmed milk for one day. I think this was on a Thursday. Well, I noticed he was standin' in the middle of the fruit juice aisle in the store with a faraway look in his eyes.

"Barney, darlin', what are you thinkin' about?" I asked.

"I'm tryin' to decide what kind of juice I'll drink Sunday!"

Cora, I hope you and Homer are fine. Take time from your busy retirement day and let us hear from you. Okay?

I go like a chicken with my head cut off half the time, but I still take time to remember my friends with a letter ever once in a while. You could do the same. Instead of lolling in the sun today, write me a letter. That would be much better for your health. I never heard of anybody gettin' skin cancer from writin' to their friends, have you?

Gotta go.

Love,
Myrtle

Barney's Dream

Dear Mr. Higgins,

It's been a while since I wrote you and you'll be pleased to know it's 'cause I've been so very busy workin' in our store. We've rented out the café and now devote all our attention to the store and to each other, of course. You'd like our store, Mr. Higgins, 'specially since you're such a sharp storekeeper.

However, our store is quite different from yours. We don't offer furniture and carpet and so on like you do. But we do offer just about everything there is in the hardware line. Barney spends half his life orderin' hard to find items. I spend half mine tryin' to figure out how to pay for 'em, but that's beside the point. I might add that we also offer our customers the convenience of shoppin' for groceries in "Barney's Place". This saves 'em from havin' to run into town so often.

Life is strange, Mr. Higgins. Barney's dream of ownin' a hardware store has finally come true. I helped his dream come true. That makes me so happy. Somebody asked me if I had a dream and outta the blue I said, "Yes, I do. I want to be a writer. Lord have mercy, Mr. Higgins, all I've ever done was write letters but for some reason I want to write more than letters. You know, somethin' that might lift the spirits of people in need of a smile-maybe shut-ins and such.

Mr. Higgins, I won't be comin' back to Florida since our business has took hold, but I do 'preciate the fact that you told me I could have my old job back. That meant a lot to me and Barney.

Oh, well, I'll keep you posted on this new adventure of mine and Barney's.

I trust your business is doing well. Give my ex-co-workers my regards.

Your friend,
Myrtle Bridges

White Knuckles

Dear Cora,

I've had you on my mind, honey, but my world has been in a topsy-turvy state lately so you've not heard from me. Let me tell you what happened since last time I wrote to you. Mama, Sissy and Aunt Fern was up to see me a while back. Aunt Fern lives in California and wanted to come up from Charlotte to the mountains while she was visitin' in N.C.

I love her to death and wanted to take her sightseein' so we got up very early in the mornin' and headed out. I drove Barney's van 'cause Sissy acted like she didn't want to drive her car. She'd just bought a brand new Ford.

When Aunt Fern saw the New River, she had a fit. She had just read a book about it so we got a two -hour book report as we rode along.

You'd love Aunt Fern. She don't talk like us but I can't hold that against her.

Around five o'clock, we headed back to my house and "the girls" started gettin' ready to go home to Charlotte. When, low and behold, Mama fell in my house and broke her hip! Cora, this might near broke my heart. I was tired from drivin' all day but me, Sissy and Aunt Fern had to drive to Charlotte late that night 'cause they took Mama to a Charlotte hospital in the ambulance so's she could have surgery close to home.

"Who's gonna drive?" Sissy asked, as we loaded up the car. "Surely, not me," I thought. I'd been drivin' all day.

Aunt Fern said she wasn't used to drivin' in the mountains. Sissy announced, "I can't see how to drive at night."

She handed me the keys to her Ford and said, "Here you go, Myrtle. I wouldn't let just anybody drive my brand new car. Be careful."

"Okay, I'll drive but, girls," I said, "don't fall asleep on me."

Aunt Fern started talkin' and might near covered ever major event in her life. She went through her widowhood and at least fifty years of livin' in California. She's been in earth quakes and I don't know what all. But, bless her heart, she kept me and Sissy awake for quite a while.

At least, I thought I was awake. Let me tell you what I did. You be the judge. I was cruisin' along makin' good time when I noticed a coffee shop up ahead on the opposite side of the road.

"Girls, let's stop for some coffee, you want to?" I said. They didn't answer 'cause they was asleep.

Cora, don't ask me why, 'cause I don't know why, but when I got directly in front of the coffee shop, instead of goin' by it and turnin' left in the proper lane, I turned smack dab in front of it and run up on the median strip! Did not wait to get to the turnin' lane!

Aunt Fern hollered, "Lord, she's gone to sleep."

"No, Aunt Fern, I ain't asleep. I'm wide awake. At least, I am now," I said.

Sissy screamed, "Myrtle, what in the world are you doin'? This ain't a turnin' lane. You jumped the median strip. "

"Sissy, I don't know why I did this. I saw the coffee place and just turned. It's as simple as that," I answered. "I know full well that one don't jump across a concrete slab when one wants to get across the road, okay?"

"Besides, I didn't jump the median strip, thank you very much, we're straddlin' it, and it's not all my fault. If you two had stayed awake and talked to me, this wouldn't have happened."

There we set, straddlin' that concrete slab when Aunt Fern said, "Well, I hope that deputy that's standin' in there usin' the phone ain't lookin' this way, but I bet he's callin' for a backup and wrecker this very minute. Hmmm, I wonder if he's married?"

"We have more important things to think about right now than that deputy's marital status, Aunt Fern," I snapped.

Sure enough, there he stood and there set two police cars in the parkin' lot. And there we set like a seesaw and Aunt Fern said, "What on earth are you gonna do, Myrtle?"

"Well," I answered, "there ain't nothin' comin'. If we ain't stuck on here, I'm gonna drive off just like I drove on—nice and easy." And that's what I did, too. With just a little bounce, we slid off and I drove into the parkin' lot like nothin' unusual had happened. I was prayin' I wouldn't hear metal fallin' off Sissy's new car. Evidently, the deputy didn't see us settin' on the median strip. If he did, he didn't let on. I couldn't believe this, but when we had rested and had our coffee and waffles and headed back to the car, Aunt Fern politely climbed in the back seat just like nothin' had happened. And Sissy got in on the passenger's side up front.

"Do ya'll want me to drive the rest of the way?" I asked. They said that they wasn't afraid of my drivin' and that I was doin' fine. I'm sure they prayed for angels to ride with us the rest of the way, though. I did.

"We all make mistakes, Myrtle, dear," Aunt Fern said. " You are truly a good driver." But then, a cousin told me later that Aunt Fern told her she rode with "white knuckles" all the way to Charlotte!

Come see us when you can. We'll go sightseein' but don't worry. Barney can do the drivin'.

Love, Myrtle,
your friend forever

Back Room Varmint

Dear Bernice,

Honey, you have been on my mind so much this week. I wish I was the nature lover you are. If I was, I wouldn't be under such stress right now. Don't get me wrong. I love nature. I just don't love all creatures the way you do.

But you must remember that Hunter helped you get over bein' afraid of any live and crawlin' varmints. He wasn't afraid to stroll around in the Everglades one bit. And you wasn't scared to touch any of them critters that lived in the glades.

Remember how brave you was when Hunter brought "Henry" home. I couldn't believe my eyes when you come walkin' in the room holdin' that half-grown iguana up like you was showin' off a new baby!

And remember how he'd run loose in the house after he realized he was like one of the family?

When I'd visit you, I never knew if he was plopped up on the window sill or behind the very chair I was settin' in.

I'll never forget the time "Henry" ran away from home and how sad you was. Then one mornin' you heard a scream that rocked the neighborhood when "Henry" had been discovered by a woman hired to wash windows next door.

That woman thought you had plum lost your mind when you went runnin' over and grabbed "Henry" up, commenced to kissin' him and sayin', "Henry, baby, are you all right?"

Bernice, I never told you this, honey, but you should have been a little concerned for the woman. I bet she was on the verge of having a biggie heart attack. I would've been.

My goodness, I don't know how I got off talkin' about "Henry". Oh, yes, I was tellin' you about my stress. Bernice, there's a snake in our stockroom. It's not my imagination either. He's been spotted. I ain't like you. I can't go in there relaxed anymore. I know he's there and he knows I know he's there 'cause when I have to go in there my head's like it's on a swivel and I'm constantly watchin' for him. And I just know, in my heart, that he's high up on a shelf lookin' down on me and probably thinkin', "That woman's got a real problem holdin' her head on."

I heard that snakes don't like mothballs so I got brave and went back there and put a few around. While I was doin' that, I heard this racket like it was hailin' and turned to see Barney throwin' mothballs out like grass seed. He had heard the same thing I had.

I said, "Barney, I followed you to Florida. I followed you to the mountains. I'm doin' my best to learn the hardware business. But Barney, darlin', I ain't workin' in no snake pit! There's a limit to what God expects of me as your wife."

I shouldn't said that 'cause he's just as much scared of that snake as I am. I don't know what come over me, Bernice. I guess it was fear! I ain't namin' that snake either, 'cause I don't want him to think he's one of the family.

Anyways, that's why you've been on my mind so much. When I go in the backroom I'll say, "What would Bernice do?" I know that you'd walk in there, get what you need, and not give it a thought. And I'll try to remember, like you say, that snake is more scared of me than I am of it.

Oh, I wish I could believe that.

I have work to do so I'll close for now.

Your friend forever,
Myrtle

Medicinal Butterflies

Dear Rose,

Thank you so much for our anniversary card. I don't know how you remember all the family birthdays and anniversaries.

Speakin' of cards, Rose, did I ever tell you about the time I sent a card to one of our customers and got embarrassed about it later? The card didn't bother me none, but what I sent with it did.

Well, to begin with, I didn't know this woman good at all, but I liked her and her husband. They have a house up here, kind of like a vacation home, 'cause they live down the mountain most of the year.

Anyways, to make a long letter short, one day here comes the man in the store but his wife wasn't with him. I don't like to appear to be nosey, mind you, but I did wonder where she was, so's I just come out and said, "Where's your wife?"

"She's up at the house. She was in an accident and can't get around yet," he answered.

"Mercy, I'm so sorry," I said. "Let me send her a get well card. You don't mind takin' it to her, do you?"

"No, not at all, " he answered.

I started to put her name on the card but I didn't know it, so's I said," What's her name, anyways?"

"Her name is Levern," he told me. "And my name is A.T."

Well, I addressed Levern's card and remembered how she always bought peanut brittle candy when she'd come in the store, so I grabbed a little paper sack and filled it with peanut brittle and orange slices. One thing just led to another and I picked out some little butterfly magnets and put them in the bag with the card. I figured she could stick 'em on her fridge.

"Here," I said, as A.T. was gettin' ready to leave. "Give this bag of goodies to Levern and tell her Myrtle sent 'em to her and I hope she feels better soon."

I bet it wasn't two hours before Levern called to thank me for the "sunshine" bag.

"How'd you like them butterflies?" I asked.

"How did you know that I love butterflies?" she said. "I stuck 'em on my fridge. They're darlin'."

We talked for a spell and she said she'd be in to see me just as soon as she got to feelin' better.

Now, you might be thinkin', "What's so odd about that, Myrtle?"

I'll tell you what's odd about it, Rose. I found out later that Levern was a doctor! When I found out that she was a doctor, the first thing I thought of was them eighty-nine cent butterfly magnets. Actually, three of 'em cost eighty-nine cents. They was flittin' around right before my very eyes, in my mind, so to speak.

Rose, when was the last time you give a doctor eighty-nine cent stick-ons?

I got to thinkin' about it though, and remembered how nice she was to call to thank me, and then, I didn't feel so bad. She didn't have to do that. We've become real friends now and you'd be surprised just how much we have in common.

For instance, we're the same age, we've both had one husband, one son and two daughters. And get this: In 1976, the very same thing happened to Levern that happened to me. We changed careers! Levern become a doctor, and I become, well, I become a waitress. Ain't it wonderful?

Our friendship taught me this too. Don't be ashamed to do little things to cheer people up, if you get the notion. If I hadn't sent Levern the "sunshine bag" we might never have got to know each other like we did and that would of been awful.

Levern helped me to realize this: Doctors are people, too. Before Levern come along, I never thought of 'em as bein' regular folks. But she is.

I reckon the moral of this letter is to be yourself and do what you can to lift somebody's spirits. Rose, I think that's what I'm supposed to do with my life. But the good part is, when I try to lift other people's spirits, I lift my own!

Oh well, I'd better close for now. Thanks again for the card.

Love,
Myrtle

Lavender Lace

Dear Bernice,

How in the world are you? I've not had the good fortune of hearin' from you lately so I'm trustin' that you're fine and dandy.

Me and Barney's fair to middlin'. I'm tryin' to rest up from the trip we took last week to Darlington, S.C. to see one of them car races.

Barney talked me into goin' with him. I'll swannee; I still can't resist that man. The last time he talked me into goin' to S.C. was when we eloped.

"Go with me, Myrtle," he says. "We'll have fun."

Now car racin' is lots of fun for many people. I try so hard to have fun at a race, but it ain't easy. I tell you this 'cause I know it won't go no farther. It might hurt Barney's feelin's if he knew this, and I wouldn't do that for the world, but my day was a far cry from fun. Let me tell you 'bout it and see what you think.

The day started off just as sweet as could be and ended the same way, but the in-between part was a killer. We left very early and stopped for breakfast in a quaint little restaurant and watched the sunrise, which was lovely. It amazes me how new and beautiful something as old as the sun can look everday.

Anyways, after we got to the track and parked the car, we had time to kill, so we took a long walk and found a chicken place and ate lunch. Up to this point, everthing was fine and cozy 'cause I loved bein' with Barney. We even held hands as we walked along. But when we walked back to the track and located our seats, we was in for more cozy than I had bargained for.

Our seats was made outta metal and the sun had been bearin' down on 'em so they was hotter than a bonfire. Barney had to make sure we'd get in our seats in plenty of time to hear them gentlemen start their engines so we sat there broilin' for at least a hour just anticipatin' the start of the race. I used this time to people watch. There was plenty of 'em to watch, too, believe me.

It's no wonder they call that place Darlington. There's surely a ton of darlin's prancin' around. One of 'em pranced in front of us to get to her seat and you ain't gonna believe this but she had on a tee shirt and that's all. If she had on anything under that shirt, I sure bud couldn't see it and I looked hard. The only thing hangin' out from under that shirt was the parts of her body that shoulda been covered! Barney said she had a bathing suit on under the shirt. He musta looked harder than me.

I said to Barney, "How in the world can she set down on that hot seat?"

He grinned and said, "I don't know but I'm gettin' a shot of it with my camera when she tries." He then proceeded to get her in focus. That didn't bother me none 'cause I was just as curious as he was. Well, almost as curious.

Now, I'll admit that when a race starts, it's plum excitin' and I enjoy it immensely. But after watchin' them cars about ten laps around the track my mind starts to wander and I keep thinkin' of things I could be doin' at home—like washin' woodwork or cleanin' the oven.

As time drug on, somethin' hit me like a bolt outta the blue. I'd just seen a program on CNN last week about the hole in the Ozone and the dangers of skin cancer. I grabbed my bottle of sun lotion and soaked my face and arms with it. Barney refused to use any. He couldn't take his eyes off that track long enough to protect his self.

Neither could all the people sittin' around us. I all but begged one woman to use some of it. But would she? No! She was completely engrossed by that race.

Now where was I? Oh yes, sittin' in the sun. I'm ashamed to tell you this but I was so concerned about my own sufferin' that I don't remember prayin' for the safety of the drivers—even Richard Petty's! I looked around and all them people looked like the very ones I prayed for at the Bristol race, so I shut my eyes and said, "Lord, just bless 'em all." He knew my heart and knew I had left Barney's binoculars at the house so I let it go at that.

You know how the heat can get to you after a spell, don't you? It wasn't long before it got to me. Picture yourself endurin' a four hour hot flash. I was feelin' a tad sick to my stomach when that Barney reached in the leftover chicken bag and pulled out a drumstick and started munchin' on that greasy thing. I thought I'd die! I was so thankful that I hadn't fixed him some hard boiled eggs. I couldn't of stood it.

Speakin' of standin', did you know that them thousands of people pay for a seat to set in and then stand up most all of the race? Now that don't make sense to me. But I didn't care 'cause I learned quite by accident that if I just kept my seat and minded my own business when they all jumped to their feet, they caused me to be in a shadow. So you might say, "I had it made in the shade."

One time durin' a long caution period, my shade was gone and my hot flash was 'bout to get the best of me when I looked in front of us and noticed the care center. At first, I thought I was hallucinatin'. I kept thinkin' that if only I could get over there to that little buildin' with the red crosses on it, I could stretch out on a cot and have a glass of cool water. But to get there, I'd a had to cross the track after climbin' a fence and them flagmen would have black flagged me for sure.

Them men had enough to do without me addin' to their worries. They speak a flag language to them drivers, you know. You ain't never seen such wavin' in all your life. And it's down right graceful, the way they do it. They don't get a minutes rest from the time them gentlemen start their engines till the race is over. As I studied them wavin' the flags, I compared the wavin' to our life.

For instance, if we was causin' a person to have a problem, a blue flag would appear somewhere warnin' us to get out of their way so they could move ahead easier in this life. If a black flag waved we'd know we was 'bout to be chastised. A yellow flag would caution us to watch out for trouble or to slow down. If all was well and we was doin' okay, we'd have a green flag wavin' somewhere urgin' us on. Then of course, when we'd done the best we could and our race in life was over, there'd be a checkered flag lettin' us know we could stop now. We had reached the finish line.

When the winnin' car reached the finish line and the race was over and me and Barney headed home, I experienced the best part of the day. I was tryin' to relax while Barney drove and that ain't easy to do just after the race. He turns into a NASCAR driver person, or at least, he tries to.

"For goodness sakes, Barney, slow down. You're not on the race track," I said.

He did slow down, and I was enjoyin' the scenery when we come upon a section of woods where wisteria had grown over the evergreens. Barney poked along so's I could get the picture set in my mind good. I called it "Lavender Lace." That's what it looked like to me, Bernice. Beautiful lavender lace spread over the greenery of the trees. That was the highlight of the day for me—so cool and refreshin'. I wasn't expectin' to see anything so lovely. I thanked the Lord for puttin' it there too.

The trip was a good break away from work, and I'm thankful I got to go with Barney, but it's only fair that he take one of his buddies next time. In fact, I'm gonna insist on it.

Bernice, Barney just this minute told me that Trixie told him she'd loved to go to a car race sometime. In fact, his very words was, "Myrtle, did you know that sweet little Trixie has never been to a NASCAR race and she'd love to go to one?"

You might remember me tellin' you about Trixie. She's the little blonde with blue eyes the size of robin eggs that gave Barney the perm that time.

I said, "Oh, Barney darlin', let's take her with us to the very next race. You want to?"

I sure hope she's got a pair of sunglasses to cover them big blue eyes with. I'll have to remember to take a spare with me just in case she ain't. Oh well, gotta go.

Love, your friend forever
Myrtle

Sparkle's Secret

Dear Bernice,

You've been on my mind ever since I went to my family reunion. After I tell you what happened, you'll see why.

Let me start at the beginnin'. I can't stand to start in the middle, can you?

After the family finished eatin', everbody caught up on the news. Then, we started reminiscin' about Grandma and Grandpa. Now, that can take a while. First one and then the other would tell their favorite story about 'em and the memories flowed and soothed like sweet oil.

Well, I noticed my cousin Sparkle was kinda quiet and that ain't like her at all. In fact, she's usually real bubbly and the center of attention.

"Why are you so quiet, Sparkle?" I asked. "What's wrong?"

"Nothin'," she said. "I'm just listenin."

It wasn't like her to just listen either, so I said, "Come on, Sparkle. You can tell us."

"No, I can't. I've carried this baggage around for years and plan to take it to my grave."

It's been proved that one has to talk his or her problems out to maintain good health. Did you know that, Bernice? Barney says that's why I'm so healthy. I don't hold back. Anyways, let me get back to Sparkle and her secret.

"No, no, honey bunch," I said, "you've got to unload whatever it is that's botherin' you. Do you want to go inside, stretch out on the couch and talk about it?"

"When did you start practicin' psychiatry, Myrtle?" she asked. " I musta missed something."

"I've graduated from the 'school of hard knocks' and I read 'Dear Abby' faithfully, so I bet I can be of help to you, sweetie," I told her.

"Okay, but you've got to promise you won't tell a soul," she whispered. "Not Barney. Not none of your kids. Nobody."

"I won't tell 'em. But, can't I tell Bernice? I tell her might near everthing. I'd trust her with my life. Your secret is safe with me and Bernice," I assured her. So Bernice, you mustn't repeat Sparkle's confession. Okay? I promised.

"Let's take a walk and I'll try to tell you my shameful secret," Sparkle said. "It goes way back to when I was a young girl. Do you remember that old Chevy car Grandpa had?"

"No, not really," I said. "Should I?"

"How could you forget it, Myrtle?" she asked. "I'll never forget it as long as I live and you're much older than me."

"Not that much. What color was it, anyways?" I asked. I hoped that would jog my memory. That was the wrong thing to ask. Sparkle broke into tears and said, "Blue. Bright blue! His old car needed a paint job and Grandpa couldn't afford it so he bought a can of bright blue paint and a brush and painted it by hand. That old car had brush streaks and bristles stuck all over it."

"What's that got to do with you?" I asked. Curiosity was gettin' the best of me by now.

"I think of it ever time I see a blue car. Do you know how many times a week I do that?" she asked.

"So what's the problem, Sparkle?" I asked, tryin' to be of comfort.

"One day," she snubbed, "Grandpa, bless his sweet heart, offered to take me to school 'cause I had missed the bus. Myrtle, I was so ashamed to be seen ridin' in that car with him that I scooted way down in the seat and hid so nobody could see me," she said. She wasn't whisperin' no more. She stopped talkin' long enough to take a breath and drawed her shoulders up to her ears in a 'down scootin' position lookin' like a little turtle. I thought she was ready for a piece of my helpful wisdom since she thinks I'm so much older.

"That's it? You mean to stand there and tell me that's your secret?" I asked. "You tore my nerves up over that? I ain't believin' this." She didn't act like she heard me. Here she goes again. "If our grandpa was alive today, I'd proudly ride in that car with him. I'd hold my head high and wave at people. I'd even kiss him bye in front of my classmates." She was wavin' her arms and I was thinkin' how good she woulda done on Broadway!

"Sparkle, get control of yourself." To calm her down, I thought I was gonna have to slap her face like they do in the movies. "I bet Grandpa knows how you feel. You're bein' too hard on yourself, honey bunch," I told her.

"Would you a' done such a shameful thing, Myrtle?" she asked. "No, I know you wouldn't. You're a better person than I am."

"No, I'm not a better person than you are. But I wouldn't a'done what you did."

"What would you a'done?"

"I'd a probably got in the back seat and laid face down," I teased.

Sparkle's face lit up. She hugged me and said, "Thank you, Myrtle. Thank you. I needed that."

She blowed her nose and looked like the weight of the world had been lifted from her shoulders. We went back and joined the rest of the family. They hadn't even missed us. I never said a word about Sparkle's secret so keep it to yourself, Bernice.

But we can learn a lesson from it, can't we?

Much love to my friend forever,
Myrtle

A Chillin' Memory

Dear Claudine,

Camille told me that you called while me and Barney was away last week. I'm so sorry I missed your call. You know how I love talkin' to you.

We wasn't gone for long; only one night, but we sure did enjoy ourselves.

Do you remember Cora and Homer? I reckon you don't since you never had the pleasure of meetin' 'em. Anyways, they invited us over to Spruce Pine to spend the night.

They don't live there. They still live in Florida but have friends who own this condo. It's lovely and it's settin' smack dab on a golf course!

I'm hopin' I don't catch cold. The weather was nice but we come close to freezin' our first and only night there. Cora mentioned that there wasn't much covers but we'd be comfortable with the sheets and spreads that was on the beds in the guest room. Wrong.

Homer turned the air conditioner down real low before we went to bed. He said he didn't want us to be too warm. Barney swears Homer didn't want us to stay but one night. If that's the case, Homer got his wish!

Claudine, I'm here to tell you that I woke up in the night and thought I had died and gone to the North Pole. I was nearly froze to

death. For one thing, I'm used to sleeping' with Barney and didn't
have that arm of his slung over me like a burnin' log. But that wasn't
the problem. Homer had also brought Barney a fan because Barney
told him he always had a fan blowin' on us at night. He failed to tell
him that I usually had a quilt pulled up to my chin. Anyways, there I
was in that cold bed, by myself, the air conditioner set way down, with
next to no cover and with that dadburned fan blowin' on us!

"Barney, are you awake?" I whispered. He was snorin' so
loud he couldn't hear me.

"He's warmer than me," I thought, "or he'd be awake tryin' to
figure out what to do."

I wanted him to go down to the parkin' lot and get a quilt that
was in our van. Oh, how I longed for that quilt!

Claudine, you know how the bed gets real warm under your
body when you stay real still. Believe me when I say there wasn't an
inch of warmth anywhere to be found on my bed.

"On the count of three, Myrtle, jump outta this bed and shut
that fan off," I said to myself. Then, I dove back in the bed and just
laid there thinkin' about homeless people in the wintertime until Barney
woke up.

"Barney, I'm so cold my blood's like a slurpee," I told him.

"Homer got it too cold, didn't he, Myrtle? Why didn't you
crawl in bed with me?"

I looked over at that narrow bed and could picture me hangin'
on for dear life ever time he turned over.

"That's a joke, Barney. I can't wait to have a cup of pipin' hot
coffee. See if Cora's up."

I had planned to take my shower and fix up before I joined our
friends but there wasn't no way I could hit the shower in that frost
bitten condition, so I jumped in my jeans and kept my night shirt on
and ran to the kitchen for some coffee.

There they set.

"It got a little cool last night, didn't it, Myrtle?" Homer said.

"It was cool all right," I answered. "Have you checked to see
if any of the house plants froze?"

"Let's go set out on the porch, Cora, so's the sunshine can
thaw us out," I suggested.

We did and it wasn't no time till here comes Homer, like the
paparazzi, with his camera, gettin' a picture of Cora and me.

"People are sure to think the only thing I wear is this blue house coat," Cora said. "He never makes my picture when I'm posin' for it."

"Go away, Homer," I said. "We don't have on our makeup. My hair's not even combed and I ain't dressed for picture takin'. Leave us be."

He left us alone to talk and catch up. You know, Claudine, when Cora and me was young girls we always had a good time talkin' and things ain't changed a bit.

Of course, Barney and Homer do their share of talkin' too. You know, there's a song that says it all: When other friendships have been forgot, ours will still be hot. Well, most times, anyways.

I'd better close and write Cora now. I want to thank 'em for their hospitality.

Love, Myrtle,
your friend forever

Dishes From Afar

Dear Dil,

How in the world are you? I'm so proud to have a daughter-in-law that's a home economics teacher. You're such a great cook and all and know how to do everything just right when it comes to preparin' food and entertainin'.

You might be interested in somethin' I tried recently at mealtime. I decided to use my antique dishes 'cause I figure what's the use of havin' something that's hid away from view.

Anyways, my friend Melody was havin' supper with us and she's a whiz when it comes to old dishes. Knows all about 'em. So I decided to play this game to help Barney 'preciate and learn more about my antiques. Up until now, all that interests him is them old tools of his.

Anyways, where was I? Oh, yes, we're at the table gettin' ready to set down.

"Where do you want me to sit, Myrtle?" Barney asked.

"Barney, darlin, why don't you set next to that Mexican bowl?" I suggested.

"How do I know which is the Mexican bowl?" he asked.

"Sit next to the pinto beans, Barney," Melody said, tryin' to be of help without comin' across as a know-it-all.

"Why didn't you say that, Myrtle?" Barney mumbled.

"Barney, darlin'," I said, "would you please pass the bowl made in Germany?"

He got a crick in his neck from liftin' the bowls up to read the bottoms.

"Think about it, Barney," I said. "German potato salad is probably in the bowl made in Germany. This meal can be a learnin' experience, but we must let it happen."

"To tell you the truth, Myrtle, I was expectin' to eat a meal. If I'd a wanted a 'learnin' experience' I'd read a book."

"There's a platter on this table that was made in France," I proudly announced.

"Let me guess which one," Melody said. "I love this game. Would you like some cornbread, Myrtle?"

"Yes, thank you, I would," I answered.

"How'd you know she wanted the cornbread?" Barney asked.

"Well, since she didn't have bread on her plate yet, and since we didn't have French bread on the table, I just figured cornbread was on the platter made in France," Melody answered, "and I was right."

"I bet them peas are in a bowl made in England," Barney said. "Remember how all the Brits ate peas when we was there?"

"Very good, Barney. You're catchin' on," I said. "And just look at that sweet bowl with them tiny roses scattered all over. Is that not precious?"

"If you want to call it precious, Myrtle, go right ahead," he said. "I don't see it as bein' precious, but then, you don't get a thrill when you look at them old planes of mine the way I do either."

My most beautiful bowl is from Bavaria. Barney bought it for me one night when I didn't go with him to the auction, bless his heart. It's a light gray deep bowl with a silver edge and pink roses sprinkled in the bottom and up one side. To me, it's too beautiful for words. Melody's the only one who understands completely how I feel about my dishes.

Anyways, Melody knew right off the bat that dessert was in that bowl 'cause I made one of them Jell-O and cool whip dishes and she had enjoyed Bavarian cream before so that wasn't hard at all.

After we very carefully washed the dishes that night, she went through my cabinets and pointed out some dishes that I didn't know was old as the hills.

Barney still don't understand how gettin' an old bowl or platter makes me happier than gettin' a new outfit, but he ain't complainin' none.

When I told him that I'd love to go in the antique business someday specializin' in dishes, he said, "You'd never make a go of it, Myrtle."

"Why do you say that, Barney darlin'? You should have more confidence in my business ability than that," I told him.

"You'd never let one of them dishes be carried out the door. I can hear you now, 'That's a pretty bowl but look, there's a teeny weeny itsy bitsy crack in it. Not a good buy."

He's probably right. Maybe he'll brace my cabinets for me so they can stand the weight and I'll just keep 'em all.

Oh, well, give B.J. a hug for me. Write when you can.

Love,
Mama

Cora's Schedule

My dearest Cora,

Surely you have returned home to Florida by now and have settled down after a busy month of campin' and playin' golf. You and Homer must be exhausted.

Up until our recent one-night visit with you over at Spruce Pine, I thought I was a busy woman, what with my writin' and workin' in the store and all. But, that was before you gave me a detailed description of how you spend your time.

Now, let's see. On any given Tuesday, you said you play golf with Homer. But that just takes up half a day which leaves you plenty of time to rest up in the afternoon and get ready for a fun filled evening of bingo!.

Then, one afternoon a week is set aside so's you can play cards with your friends. Do ya'll play Crazy Eight? It must be a real challenge to find time to do your line dancin'. You poor baby.

Anyways, Cora, I must tell you that I'm a little jealous of you. I try not to be but I can't help myself. No, it ain't the fact that you can stroll along the beach and watch the sun rise or set ever day of the week. I can watch that right here in these wonderful mountains. It ain't the fact that you live with a fishin' pier practically right under your nose. I never did like to fish all that much.

It ain't the fact that you've got a gorgeous tan and figure from swimmin' in the pool located right there at your condo. That don't bother me. I'm happy for you. But, Cora, honey, did you have to tell me that you've got not one, but two Nissans?

Do you know how much I like them cars? Oh, I think if I was to win the lottery, I'd probably buy myself two right off the bat. One to drive down the driveway to work and one to drive to Mountain City to the bank.

But, I don't see that happenin'. Anyways, I don't know how I got off on cars. Where are my manners? I meant to just write and thank you and Homer for a lovely visit.

The Lord heard my prayers and me and Barney neither one took pneumonia from sleepin' in that igloo, I mean guest room.

I hope you're well and happy and think of me as often as I think of you. Cora, I missed you a lot after our short visit. In fact, I'd think to myself, "Wonder what Cora's doin' this very minute?"

We didn't have long enough to catch up, did we? Maybe we'll have another chance to visit again. I hope so.

Anyways, we know we're friends forever and come to think of it, that's a bigger blessin' than a driveway full of Nissans!

But, when I talk Barney into gettin' me a Nissan, I'll be sure to let you know.

Love,
Myrtle

A Drive Thru

Dear Hazel,

I do hope that you are feelin' your best these days. I keep thinkin' that I'll get down the mountain to see you but who knows when that'll be?

Ever time I mention goin' somewhere, Barney says, "Myrtle, I took you to Europe twice. What more do you want?"

I told him," That was ten years ago, Barney, for goodness sakes. How long is that supposed to hold me? I'm ready to take another trip. He thinks workin' is a means of stayin' young. I say that all work and no play makes me feel just a tad older than I should.

"It ain't like I want to leave the country," I told him.

He asked me where I wanted to go and I told him I'd like to go see Bernice.

"Oh no, Myrtle. I ain't spendin' vacation time listenin' to you two talk around the clock nonstop. You did that the last time we was there. Remember? Nope, ain't gonna do it. Besides, I'm too busy to think about takin' time off."

Well, Hazel, when he said all that, I was fit to be tied, specially the part about us talkin' nonstop. "We took time out to go to the bathroom, thank you very much," I told him.

The more I thought about it, the madder I got.

"Okay, Barney," (did not throw in a darlin' either), I think I've got a great plan for you and your work."

When I die, if it's before you die, this is what I want done. Listen up, it's important. To save you time from lost work I want our friendly undertaker to make a few exceptions for me. Don't want you to lose time from work for a viewin'. Forget that. It'd be too time consumin'. Instead, have him cart me over here and set me up out in the parkin' lot. You can keep workin' but make a big sign that reads, "Honk, if you loved Myrtle."

"That way, my friends can pay their respects without gettin' out of their cars. The viewin' can be a drive-thru and you won't have to leave the buildin'. You can stand in the doorway and wave to my friends and then jump back to the counter and wait on a customer."

Of course, I was kiddin', but I don't think Barney was when he said, "Boy, Myrtle, you know how to get a man's attention, don't you?"

I have a feelin' I might get to see Bernice before too long. I ain't told him that she's moved to Iowa yet 'cause he's plannin' on a deep sea fishing trip while me and Bernice catch up. I'll keep that bit of news for later. Like when we're in the car and he's ready to drive off to Florida.

Guess I'd better close for now. I'll keep you posted on our whereabouts.

Much love,
Myrtle

A Shinin' Moment

I ain't got time for fancy beginnin's, Bernice. I bet you can't guess what I did. But, then, you might can 'cause I told you what I was gonna do, didn't I? Lord, I'm so excited I can't think straight. Let me start all over and try to sound like a woman who's just finished high school.

My dearest Bernice,

How in the world are you? I do hope that everything is going well for you. How are Hunter and the children?

Barney and I are getting along very well. As a matter of fact, he mentioned that we should take a few days off work and come to Florida soon to visit B.J. and Dil.

Of course, I said, "Barney, I would certainly like to see Bernice if we go to Florida in the near future. It has been much too long since our last visit."

Shucks, Bernice, that ain't what I said at all. I said, "It's about time you thought of goin' to visit the kids and I ain't goin' to Florida without a promise from you that I can spend at least a day with Bernice. Thank you very much."

Now that I'm back to normal, I'll tell you about my graduation. I wish you could of been here, Bernice. It was one of the happiest moments of my life, and I've had quite a few. Like when I married Barney and when the kids was born.

Anyways, as I marched in with the other graduates, I wanted to cry. I wouldn't let myself until I spotted a young woman wipin' her eyes in front of me. I couldn't hold back, Bernice. My tears flowed, and I wondered why I had waited thirty-five years to finish school? Maybe it don't bother some people, and that's all right, that's their business, but it bothered me and I should of done something about it years ago!

Bernice, honey, I started havin' this dream over and over again. Always the same dream. I'd be with a group of friends from school days and I never had on my shoes! Never, Bernice. My friends had on shoes but not me. I knew there was a reason for this dream. You know, I stopped dreamin' it the day I went back to school to get my GED!

Have never dreamed it since. I wish I would so's I could see what kind of shoes I'm wearin'.

Anyways, back to my graduation.

The vice president of the community college gave a speech and said that he knew how hard it was for some of us to come back and finish high school late in life. What with workin' and all. He said that he was proud of us and knew that we'd all feel better about ourselves and that it would make a difference in our lives.

That night was truly a shinin' moment in my life.

You know, Bernice, finishin' school wasn't that hard to do. I took little tests at school and then, I'd study up on the subjects I needed to improve on at home before I took the big tests that really counted. The hardest part was goin' over and sayin', "I quit school years ago. Tell me what I need to do to finish now."

I'm goin' to take a writin' class now and who knows what'll happen? It seems that the more I learn, the more I want to learn. Don't that beat all? I just have this feelin', Bernice, that I'm gonna to be a writer! In my heart of hearts, I know it.

Seems like forever since I last saw you. Hope it won't be much longer till we can talk in person.

Until then, remember we're friends forever.

Love,
Myrtle

Radio Land

Dear Hazel,

Boy, have I got news for you! Do you remember the poetry contest I wrote you about? Well, I entered it and won in the "most unusual" category.

I won five dollars but you can't count that 'cause I paid five dollars to enter the contest. However, I had the privilege of readin' my poem on the radio. Can you believe that?

I marched right in the radio station and introduced myself as Myrtle Bridges, the winning poetess from North Carolina.

I reckon they could tell I was just a tad nervous so they was extra nice to me. Anyways, after my voice took on a more "professional" sound, a young woman took me to a soundproof room and showed me what to do.

"You're on your own," she said, and went outside to watch through a window from another room.

I did somethin' I've always wanted to do. I put them little earmuffs on and said, "Testin' 1-2-3, testin' 1-2-3." Then, I thanked the Lord for the day He had made and asked Him to help me get through it. I wanted my poem to sound just right and didn't want to start off cold with it, so I said, "Hello out there in radio land. This is Myrtle Bridges comin' to you taped. Well, I'm not taped—just my voice is. When ya'll hear this I won't even be here, I'll be home."

It was right about then when all them people at the station started peckin' on the window and motionin' with their hands that I should wrap it up. But since you ain't in broadcastin' like me you may not get the picture. But I got it and I hurried to introduce my poem, but first I had to tell 'em that the very last line of my poem belonged to my writin' instructor. It's a sin to use somebody else's written words as you own. Bet you didn't know that either, did you, honey?

Anyways, as I was ready to leave the station, I'd told 'em I'd never in all my life experienced a day quite like that one. They all agreed they hadn't either.

I know you're dyin' to read my poem, ain't you, Hazel? That's what I love about you. When good things happen to me, they happen to you too.

Here it is. I called my prize winnin' poem

"Aggravatin' Souls."

You know the kind
They're easy to find
Harassment's their game
Embarrassment's their aim
Pretendin' to be true blue friends
When really, they're two faced blends
Of hypocrisy and horses ends
But there'll come a day
When we can say
Now, they know how it feels
'Cause time after all, will wound all heels.

We see them "aggravatin' souls" just about everwhere we go, don't we? Guess we should pray 'em and try not to be one of 'em ourselves.

Hazel, I'm tryin' to talk Barney into havin' a Saturday mornin' radio show of our own. We've rented out the café and Barney's dream has come true to own a hardware store. We could tell people all about the hard-to-find hardware items we sell. Since he don't know as much about broadcastin' as I do and don't talk a lot either, I told him that I'd do all the talkin' but ever so often I could say, "Ain't that right, Barney?" And he could say, "Yep."

"Rocky Top" still gives me goose bumps and a lump in my throat every time I hear it so I figure it'd make a great theme song. Whatta you think? Reckon I'd better get busy and go help Barney in the store. Bless his heart, he must miss me when I'm not around.

Come up when you can.
Love, Myrtle

Danglin' by a Thread

My dear B.J.,

Would it be possible for you to come up here and help your mama learn how to use that dad-blamed computer? There ain't no way I can learn by myself.

Son, I believed you when you said, "Mama, you'll love it. It's easy as pie after you get the hang of it."

Easy as pie, my eye. I'm just about cross-eyed for your information. Not only that, I talk to myself out loud. Dern, I even talk to the computer out loud!

Last night, your dad was watchin' TV and I was tryin' my best to write a story when it asked me if I really wanted to change somethin'.

I screamed, "How do I know? And don't start flashin' that question mark in front of my face either. I'll box you up and use this desk for my books and typewriter. I'm sick of your questions, do you hear me?" I reckon I was just a tad loud 'cause you dad come runnin' over and said," Myrtle, what in the world is wrong with you? Have you lost your mind?"

"Shush up, Barney," I said. "My sanity is danglin' by a thread and I don't need any of your questions. This Apple's more than I can handle right now. Can't you see that?"

You dad said, "It can't be that hard to learn. Everybody's usin' 'em."

"I ain't everybody. You ought to know that by now," I said. "You've lived with me long enough. But here, I'll move over so's you can set down and show me how easy it is. Let them fingers of yours dance, Barney Bridges."

I realized I wasn't bein' myself so I shut it down, poured myself a cup of coffee and went in the bedroom and cried. Don't that beat all? I can't believe I cried, but I did.

Son, I miss you so much. I was all right when you was here on your visit. All the lessons you gave me seemed so easy when you was sittin' by my side. But with you nine hundred miles away, it just ain't the same. I've lost my confidence.

I wanted that computer more than anything in this world, I thought. Now, I don't know if I'll ever learn how to use it. What will your dad think? All's I know to do is give this worry to God. If He wants me to write for Him on that machine, He's goin' to have to help me learn how. But He can do that, I'm sure.

Forget about what I said about comin' back up here. I'll take my time and try harder. If I get desperate, I'll call you. You can help me over the phone, can't you?

I feel better already. Bye for now,

Love,
Mama

Southern Belle

Dear Hazel,

You know what? If God hadn't called me to be a writer, I think He'd a called me to be a telephone operator. You know why? Next to writin', I like to talk on the phone—'specially to my friend, Claudine.

She's got one of them recorders and I can talk to her just like she's settin' there in the privacy of her own home—only she's not. Use to, I'd call her just to get to hear this sweet message she says about the beautiful world and all of us in it. Oh, it's lovely.

Well, anyways, one day after I had found out I was a writer, I called her and I mean to tell you that I needed to talk to her somethin' awful. It was utterly important. When the phone stopped ringin', I was so anxious to tell her my news and here she goes with that recorded message of hers. When she finally stopped talkin' and that beeper stopped beepin', I said the ugliest thing I ever said in my life.

I don't know what come over me, Hazel. The words just spewed out of my mouth kinda like a root beer does when you drop the can right before you pop the top.

I said, "Claudine, this is Myrtle. You've got to cut out that jibber jabber. I do not have time to stand here listenin' to you describe the world and all its beauty and all of us in it! If anybody 'preciates this world and all its beauty, I do. Now call me pronto. I needed to talk to you like two hours ago. Bye.

See what I mean, Hazel? By the time she got back to me I had plum forgot what I needed to tell her, so I just told her how much I 'preciated the way she helps me with my writin' and all.

She's a writer, you know. She's been published and everything. I love to read her poems, even if some of 'em are just a tad over my head. And she's so happy. It would be wonderful to be so smart and happy all at the same time. She has lived all over the world, and I get goose bumps when I think how God moseyed her right into Zionville, North Carolina to share her smarts with me.

Anyways, we have a Writers Conference twice a month. We meet at Wendy's or Taco Bell and eat taco salad and talk and talk and then go home and write somethin' of literary importance.

Friendship is a wonderful blessin' in life. I thank God for my friends everday. Do you?

Love,
Myrtle

Battle of the Bulge

Dear Hazel,

My, but it's been a while since I wrote you. I found your last letter the other day and couldn't believe I hadn't ever answered it. I just don't get all my "need to do's" done anymore.

Anyways, in your letter, you wrote that you was takin' exercise classes and Bible study twice a week in your church. That's quite a combination—decreasin' your physical growth and expandin' your spiritual growth. I could stand to do that, Hazel.

I got to thinkin' about that and decided to do some exercisin' myself. No, I didn't join a health club or nothin' like that. I just decided to walk as much as I can and that ain't easy bein' inside the store so much. But Hazel, I figured out a way to get a real work out right in the privacy of the store.

When I'm in there by myself, I take off to walkin' fast as I can go and say to myself, "Myrtle, don't stop till somebody comes in." This is helpin' my prayer life too 'cause when I'm tired, I say, "Lord, please send somebody in here so's I can take a break." Usually He does.

One mornin' when my walkin' was gettin' borin', I got this bright idea and stacked cans of pinto beans in the middle of the aisle and jumped 'em each time I passed that way. I was doin' real good only I got a little winded. A customer come in and I tried to act like nothin' out of the ordinary was happenin' but I was pantin' just a tad. He said, "What's wrong with you, Myrtle? You look like you've been runnin'! Where's that Barney? Has he been chasin' you?"

I didn't let on like I knew what he was talkin' about and said, "He's next door in the cafe." Barney was over there eatin' and I was in the store runnin' a obstacle course and gainin' more weight than he was. That don't make sense, does it, Hazel? I've made my mind up that I'm goin' to try to slim down a little bit and look more like the Myrtle that Barney married. Don't get me wrong. He don't say too much about the way I look and it's a good thing he don't. After all, a young bride is bound to change some after three babies and six grand young'uns and 48 years. He should expect that, don't you think?

Why is it that a woman tends to look older and a man just looks more mature when the agin' process kicks in? I reckon if they'd suffered labor pains, cramps, PMS and hot flashes like a woman, they wouldn't age so dadburn gracefully. The men look more distinguished and women look more plump. Oops, I'd better get control and think happy thoughts. They tend to keep us more youthful, don't you agree, Hazel? Happy thoughts, that is.

Oh, well, I'd better stop for now. I need to do my exercise. I think I'll concentrate on my double chin tonight. I sure wish I could relocate one of 'em.

Come up to see us soon.

Love,
Myrtle

Sloan McGuire

Dear Bernice,

I might as well write you a letter. At least, there's a chance that I'll get a reply from you. I've just about give up on ever gettin' one from Sloan McGuire. I'm so tired of waitin' for the mailman to bring me what I'm waitin' on.

I'd better start at the beginnin' so's you'll understand what I'm talkin' about.

Bernice, I bought this little book that was supposed to tell me everthing there is to know about gettin' published. I read that book twice and did exactly what it said.

I wrote a story and sent it to this Entertainment Editor named Sloan McGuire. I put my name on the first page. I doubled spaced. I didn't erase. I retyped it eighteen times to get it right. I enclosed a SASE. That means I put plenty of postage on a return envelope with my name and address on it so's Sloan McGuire could send it back to me at my expense to tell me how much he liked it and when he wanted to publish it.

I am tired of runnin' down to the mailbox and gettin' disappointed when I don't see a envelope with my writin' on it. It's awful, Bernice. I'm afraid I can't hold up under such writer's pressure.

Barney says I'm too anxious 'cause it takes a while to hear from one of them editors. He even went so far as to say, "Some people never hear from 'em, Myrtle."

Can you believe that? Well, I know it takes a while. I expected it to, but how long should it take, really? It's been two whole weeks! That's right, Bernice, two long weeks.

I tried to figure out how long it should take and I come up with one week, at the most. That's allowin' two days for it to get there, one day for him to read it, one day for him to decide to publish it, two days for his reply to get back to me. That's only six days but I give him one extra day to play around with. He's had plenty of time, don't you think? I forgot to put my phone number on the first page. He could of called me and saved so much time if I'd of just done that.

I don't want to send my story anywhere else 'cause if the second editor decided to publish it and Sloan McGuire had turned it down and happened to read it, he'd be sicker than a dog and I just couldn't do that to him.

I don't know what to do. I never dreamed that bein' a writer would be this frustratin'. It's changin' my whole life, Bernice. It's changin' Barney's life, too.

The other night, I hurried and put supper on the table. Seems like all's I ever do is hurry so's I can write. Anyways, I pushed all my writin' books down to one end of the table since I knew I'd be usin' 'em as soon as supper was over with.

Barney said, "Myrtle, where's the place mats?"

"Well, I don't know, Barney," I said, as I looked around for 'em. I couldn't find 'em so I didn't do a thing in this world but rip out a sheet of typing paper and slid it under his plate right fast like.

He didn't say nothin' but I'm sure he don't understand the "new Myrtle". Later, I found the place mats under my stack of "Writer's Digest" at the end of the table.

Now that I'm learnin' how to use my computer, when I walk in the door at night, I feel like a "magnetic force" is drawin' me in its direction so's I can write. It's spooky, Bernice. I wouldn't tell this to nobody but you. Well, I take that back. I told Claudine, but that's all. But then, I did tell my boy, B.J., but he knew it already 'cause the same thing happened to him.

Anyways, it's like I've got this new little person in me that keeps givin' me literary ideas. This same little person is givin' me courage to let people read what I write too. That's where Sloan McGuire comes in.

I even called Claudine and asked her to have her husband, Dillard, listen to the obits on the radio. I don't have the heart to listen. I'm afraid somethin' terrible has happened to Sloan and that's why I've not heard from him.

I'll let you know what develops. Remember Sloan in your prayers, just in case somethin' s wrong with him. Pray that I'll have more patience, 'specially with Sloan. Pray that Barney'll have more patience, 'specially with me.

I'll hurry and run this letter to the mail box. Maybe, just maybe, I'll have a letter from "you know who" today.

Love,
Your friend forever, Myrtle

Gone With the Wind

Dear Mama,

I've been doin' some extensive research lately but hadn't found what I'm lookin' for.

I'd write and ask the President about this but he's got so much on him right now I can't bear to burden him with my problems. However, I bet his wife could help me if I knew how to get through to her.

Since you know so much about things, I hope you can help me find the answer to my question.

Now, Mama, I know the man is supposed to be the head of the house. I've read it many times myself. I don't have a problem with that idea. But I wonder if they don't take advantage of their authority over us just a tad?

I've asked you all kinds of questions in my life, Mama, and you've always had the answer and could even show it to me in the Bible sometimes. I hope you can help me now. Not just me, Mama. I think most all the women of America need help on this. Here goes.

Mama, just where is it wrote down that the husband should be in charge of the remote control? I'm not the only woman in this world who's had no experience changin' channels. I've decided that a husband would druther have us change our mind than change a channel when he's home.

To prove my point, picture this national scene: Hubby and wife are watchin' TV. Wife loves program. Phone rings. Wife leaves room to answer phone (we have to do that too) and hurries back to finish watchin' program. That program has "gone with the wind", so to speak.

Worse, yet, it can disappear durin' a commercial. Before the commercial, wife can be watchin' a tearjerker movie and ever so fast like, that channel gets switched unbeknownst to her and when the program returns, a ballgame is on, just like it had been there all the time! Or some stranger is pullin' a big bass out of Lake Okeechobee and husband sits there in his own little world so interested that wife hates to complain.

Half the time TV's not worth watchin' anyways. I'd just as soon be at my computer, but I feel it's my duty to bring this problem up on behalf of all the women of America, don't you, Mama? I know, in my heart, that the numbers are great. But I'll wait till I hear from you to see if you think I'm over-reactin' before I send a letter to the editor.

Come to think of it, I'm happy Barney's home with me at night, even if he does hang on to that remote control. I can only hold one of his hands at a time anyways.

I'm beginnin' to see this in a different light and feel much better now. Forget what I said.

What would I do without you, Mama? Or Barney?

Love,
Myrtle

Dearest Aunt Fern,

Thank you for that postcard from the Big Apple, also known as New York City. Mercy, you musta had a good time tourin' this summer.

You wanted to know if we'd been on any tours lately and the answer is no. Well, I take that back. Me and my friend, Julia, did tour Ashe County last year. But, that tour wasn't planned. Let me tell you about it.

You see, Julia is a writer like me, and we drove over to Ashe County to go to a writers meetin'. You just can't learn too much about writin', you know. Anyways, we both had been there before, but not together at the same time. A writer has to be so careful to make everthing they, I mean, he or she, writes come out plain as day so's the reader don't have to guess at what's bein' said. I've already learned a bunch, don't you think?

Now, this is where the tourin' started. When we left the meetin', I got the bright idea to take Julia by *The Mountain Times* office so's she could meet the folks there. Did not have one bit of trouble gettin' there either.

When we left the Times, I thought I was headed in precisely the same direction that I had come into town, but goin' the opposite way, of course.

Well, I'm here to tell you, I wasn't. We started climbin' a hill- one I hadn't seen before.

"Julia, do you feel like you've ever been on this road," I asked.

"I was just thinkin' about that, Myrtle," she said. " I've never been on this road in my life, but ain't the scenery lovely?" And it was lovely and it got lovelier each time I'd go up it! Why, I commenced to feelin' like I was on my way to visit relatives!

"Julia," I said, "what am I doin' wrong here?"

"Don't get excited, Myrtle. We know there's a way outta here 'cause when we rode into Ashe County, it was easy as pie."

Julia's always comparin' somethin' to food. She's not only a writer, but she's a great cook, too, and even wrote a cookbook.

Anyways, I said, "You pick which way I should turn."

"Okay, I choose this way," she said, pointin' her finger to the left. I know full well that she had said, "Eenie, meenie, minie, moe" to make her choice, but I didn't say a word. I turned. Beautiful scenery, at least, but not any that looked familiar.

We passed the driver's license place. "I could swear we've past this buildin' before," Julia said. "If not, what are they doin' with so many different locations?"

"Surely it's the same one. If it's not, the governor needs to know about this and Ashe County should downsize just a tad. Three driver's license examiners is too many for any county, don't you agree, Julia?" I asked.

"I do, Myrtle," she said. And in my heart, I know she was thinkin' "Wonder where Myrtle got her license to drive?" Or, "Wonder if Myrtle even has a license? I didn't think to ask before I got in her car. Wish I had."

"Watch out for a gas station," I said. "We don't want to run outta gas on the way home, that is, if we ever get headed in the right direction."

"What time did you tell Barney we'd be back?" Julia asked.

"I didn't think to mention that, thank the Lord," I answered.

"Good. Then, it won't give him cause for concern that it's startin' to get dark, will it?"

"Well, it's givin' me cause for concern", I said. "Do you want to drive?"

"Oh no, Myrtle, you're doin' fine. You know, we could stop and ask somebody for directions," she said.

" They'd think we didn't know how to get to Watauga County, Julia," I said. "I don't want 'em to think that."

"Why? We don't know?" she answered.

I knew it. She knew it, but I didn't want the world to know it. Anyways, quite by accident, we came to a spot we both recognized and both of us shouted for joy and headed back home all in the same day. So, Aunt Fern, that's about all the tourin' I've done lately. Thanks for your invitation to come out to California to visit. I asked Julia if she'd like to drive out there with me.

"Myrtle, you've got to be kiddin," she said. "It'd take us two years to get to California and back. I can't be gone that long."

So, I guess I won't be comin' to see you but I do hope you'll get to come visit us sometime this year.

I send my love,
Myrtle

At the Sound of the Beep

Dear Bernice,

    I bet you knew this letter was in the mailbox before you checked the mail, didn't you? You've been on my mind so much lately. I'd give a pretty if it wasn't long distance to call you. Someday I want to talk to you like we use to do-just girl talk-you know- no special reason just sharin' our dreams and all. Sometimes we'd talk at least twice a day. Anyways, I don't do that no more. Most of my phone calls to friends here are short and to the point—so to speak.

    For instance, when I call my friend Claudine, I most always get her recordin' and have to hurry and leave my message. Since she's been published and all, I ask her for advice regardin' my writin'. She's such a help when I can catch her off guard and she picks up the phone before she realizes what she's doin'. I called her three times today and hadn't made direct contact yet.

    I mean, I waited 'til 8:00 this mornin' to call her. I'd been up two hours so I figured surely she was up and at 'em. But did she have the courtesy to answer the phone in person? No! Instead, I had to listen to her message again before I could get in my two-cents worth. The conversations went like this.

    Claudine, this is Myrtle. This friendship business is a two-way street, and you don't have to wait to call me simply to return one of my many calls. What's wrong with pickin' up the phone and callin' to say, "Hello, Myrtle, this is Claudine"? I was thinkin' 'bout you bein's we're such good friends and all. How are you today, anyways?" But since you didn't do that, Claudine, I'll tell you. I'm fine. Bye.

    Claudine, this is Myrtle. Our Writers Conference will be at Wendy's this week on Thursday at eleven o'clock. Please try to attend. I do not like to eat alone. Bye.

    Claudine, this is Myrtle. Why in the world don't you just get up out of that bed and answer your phone? I know you're home. I hope when I get published, I won't let it go to my head like some people do. I plan to stay just like I am now—available for all my friends whenever they need to talk to me. I'm listed in the book in case you've lost my number again. Bye.

    Well, that's how my phone calls went today. I may try once more and if she don't answer I might just go up the mountain to see her in person. I've got to ask her what a query letter is? Why on earth would one deliberately send a query letter to anybody? Seems like a waste of time to me. Don't you agree? And it don't sound too nice either.

Bernice, I sure feel like we've had one of our visits only you've just been listenin'. You always was a good listener come to think of it. I miss you, Bernice. Remember, we're friends forever.

Love,
Myrtle

Words of Wisdom

Dear Claudine,

After I met you and we hit it off as friends, I felt sure that we'd grow old together. That's what friends do, ain't it?

But, come to think of it, I always thought me and Bernice would grow old together too, down in Florida. And I upped and moved away, leavin' that sweet girl down there to face agin' without me. I know now how she felt.

It hurts, Claudine. I know in my heart that God sent you to Zionville to direct my new found writin' career. I never dreamed He'd lead you in another direction after you done it.

Camille said to me, when I was gettin' emotional about your soon -to- be departure, "My word, Mama. Claudine ain't dying. She's only movin'. She's alive and well. Be thankful for that."

Camille's words of wisdom helped me to think happier thoughts and I'm goin' to share 'em with you.

I'm writin' you this letter to tell you what you mean to me. We have laughed together and shed tears together that have bonded our friendship forever.

It won't matter one bit if you're here or somewhere else. We'll always be best of friends. Like I told Bernice-I'll only be a thought away. Don't ever forget that.

I felt it my duty to write a poem for you bein's you're leavin' and all. Besides, I have several of your lovely poems to treasure and want you to have one of mine. I called it **CLAUDINE.**

> **C** is for the wooden cross I gave you
> **L** is for the laughter you gave me
> **A** is for the angels that surround you
> **U** is for your universal love

D is for the dove so symbolic of your ways
I is for the insight that you gave me
N is for the nerve you gave me too
E is for the exit you are taking
And I'd like to know what in the world am I supposed to do? Excuse me, Claudine, I didn't mean to say that. It just slipped out.

Put them all together they spell **Claudine**, my friend forever.

I hope you like it. Since you write such lovely poetry, I'm anxious to see what kind of letters you write.

Love,
Myrtle, your friend forever

Preventive Measures

Dearest Hazel,

I am so upset right now that I may not be able to write this letter but I'm gonna try 'cause it's been proved that we must rid ourselves of frustrations if we are to remain happy in this world. And talkin' 'bout 'em helps to remove 'em. Frustrations, that is.

Never in all our years of marriage has Barney Bridges embarrassed me as much as he did today. I was dustin' the shelves in the store. My little feather duster was dancin' all over the baby items and I was just a singin' "One little, two little, three little Indians" when a man customer walked down the aisle and stopped to talk to me. I stopped singin', of course, and turned to help him.

Now picture this: I'm standin' there with my back to the baby notions but the feather duster was still in my hand on top of a box of diapers. At least, I thought it was on a box of diapers. I noticed the man lookin' past me as though he was readin' or somethin'. I turned to see what he was lookin' at and might near fainted!

There sat a giant box of preventive measures, if you know what I mean. I jumped square in front of 'em so's he couldn't see 'em and said, "Are you lookin' for Barney?"

"No, I think I found what I'm lookin' for, if you'll excuse me." And with that, he reached around me and got him a handful of protection.

Thank goodness, Barney was at the register so I didn't have to ring him up. As soon as the man left, I snatched that box off the shelf and marched up to Barney and screamed, "What in the world do you mean by puttin' these things with the baby items? Are you crazy?"

"Why do you say that?" he asked. "I can't think of a better place for 'em. It'll remind people to buy 'em so they won't be buyin' diapers forever."

"Barney," I said. "I am not workin' in this store if these things are left on that shelf."

"Where do you suggest they go?" he asked.

"I don't know but I'll find a place. Don't you worry," I said.

"Myrtle, you're too much," he muttered and just shook his head.

Well, I carried them things around tryin' to work 'em in somewhere so's they'd not cause embarrassment to me or any of the ladies that come into the store. I found the perfect spot, too—sandwiched in between two boxes of tobacco.

I can't take but so much stress in one week. Surely to goodness that'll be the end of that. But if I was to catch 'em back on the baby shelf, I'm retirin' from the store business to become a full time wife and homemaker. But as Barney would say, "That'll be the day."

Thanks for lettin' me get this off my chest. I feel much better, thank you.

Love,
Myrtle

Auction Fever

Dear Claudine,

It's been quite a while since I wrote to you, I know, but I keep on the go so much, you'd be sure to understand if you was here with me.

Just as sure as the sun's gonna set on Friday night, me and Barney's goin' to a auction. No matter how hard we worked that day or how tired we are, we're gonna hop in that car and head for Tennessee!

I'll say, "Barney, darlin', are we goin' to the auction tonight?"

And he always says, "I don't know, Myrtle, we might," knowin' full well he wouldn't miss one for all the tea in China! Talk about addiction!

Have you ever been to one, Claudine? At first, I was bashful and wouldn't bid on nothin'. But Barney, he ain't never been bashful when it come to biddin'. You wouldn't believe the stuff he's bought. He loves the old timey tools. I love the old dishes.

I have to pay attention to what I'm doin' 'cause I see so many of our customers there and I can't be friendly, Claudine, and wave at 'em. I learned that the hard way. I have a problem with not wavin'.

To prove my point, one night I was lookin' around and seen a friend of ours and not wantin' to be snooty, I waved and said," Hey, Ernie."

Claudine, I come close to buyin' somethin' I didn't want, cause when I waved at Ernie, I was biddin' $9.00 on a snow tire unbeknownst to me. It was ten minutes before I'd make eye contact with the auctioneer again. Thank goodness, somebody raised my bid and went home with that snow tire.

Now, if my nose starts itchin', I just let it itch! You can't be too careful, Claudine. Any sudden moves can be costly.

But then, Yvonne was with us one night and you wouldn't believe what she did to me.

Well, first of all, do you remember how I dearly love angels? Well, here comes two angel candle holders up for bid and I'm here to tell you I wanted 'em. They was beautiful.

"I'm biddin' on them," I proudly told Yvonne. And I did 'til the price shot up higher than I wanted to pay.

"Mama, you know you want them angels," Yvonne said. With that, she took hold of my hand and shot it up in the air! I could not believe she did that. Not once, but twice. I fixed her. I set on my hand and she couldn't pry it out from under me but she throwed her own hand up and bid on 'em. Needless to say, them beautiful blue angel candle holders are sittin' on my piano right now, thanks to Yvonne and Barney. He paid for 'em. Did not complain one bit. But how could he? He bought a corn sheller and don't even have a garden. At least, I've got candles.

Give all the family our love and come up to see us. But, if it's on a Friday night, we'll most likely be auctionin'. So plan to go with us.

Love,
Myrtle

Bullseye

Dear Bernice,

Well, here I am wantin' to talk to somebody and there ain't nobody around. Barney went to one of them car races. I could of gone with him if I wanted to. Instead, I said, "Barney, darlin', you just go on without me. I don't mind one bit. Besides, my hearin' just now got back to normal after goin' to that last race."

I would call Camille tonight but she ain't talkin' to me right now. I take that back. Today she did say, "Mrs. Bridges, the phone's for you." I can't see why in the world she's so mad at me. I mean, accidents happen. Well, the accident's not the reason she's mad. The way I reacted to the accident is why she's mad.

Let me start at the beginnin' and see what you think about it.

Camille decided to mop the store floor today so I got my broom and started sweeping' just ahead of her so the floor would be nice and clean where she mopped.

She had the mop water good and sudsy and while we worked, we was havin' one of our mother-to-daughter talks and everthing was peachy.

Well, I looked back at Camille just as she plopped her mop into the bucket and proceeded to squeeze the water out of it. Then, she lifted the mop upwards just a tad to clear the bucket and lo, and behold, that mop handle bumped the galvanized bucket that was hangin' from the ceiling' precisely above her head!

Are you gettin' the picture? I saw what was about to happen and tried to warn her but it was too late. That bucket dropped smack dab on her head! Centered it like a hat and bounced off just like one of them video bouncin' balls. If you could of seen the look on her face, you'd done exactly what I did, which was laugh. But then, maybe I didn't laugh till the yellow plastic bucket dropped too, hit and followed the same path as bucket #1. I figured the vibration of bucket #1 caused bucket #2 to drop. Honestly, Bernice, I tried with all the powers in me not to laugh but I couldn't help myself.

For one thing, at first, she was so shocked she couldn't speak. But I could tell she was thinkin', "I ain't believin' this. I've just been hit on the head with not one, but two buckets!!"

Finally, when I could halfway speak, I said, "Camille, honey, are you all right?"

"Don't Camille, honey, me," she hollered. "I can't believe you thought that was funny!" And she took off to the back room with me right on her heels.

"Where're you goin', Camille?" I questioned.

"Where do you think I'm goin'? I'm tryin' to get away from you!" she might near screamed.

I tried to reason with her but that's hard to do when one is bent over laughin'. Bernice, I don't know what come over me. I couldn't stop it and I felt terrible. Finally, I got control of myself long enough to say, "Where's your sense of humor, Camille?"

"It sure ain't in that bucket," she hollered, and proceeded to shut the door practically in my face! And would have if I hadn't blocked it with my foot. I'm still walkin' with a limp.

Anyways, she said, "Just leave me alone, mama."

"Watch your mouth, young lady," I said, "you're just a hair away from sassin' me. Don't forget I carried you for nine long months."

"And I bet my delivery was a real hoot, wasn't it?" she snapped.

I limped off back to the counter that had five people, all ears, standin' in line to be waited on.

Oh, well, by mornin' she'll be okay. She's like her mama. She don't stay mad for long. Life's too short for that.

Bernice, writin' you was almost as good as talkin' to you. Write back when you can.

Love,
Myrtle, your friend forever

A Piece of Cake

Dear Bernice,

Did you think I fell right off the face of the earth or what?

I said to Barney, "Mercy, I'm so far behind in my letter writin' I'll never catch up."

He said, "Oh, you'll manage, Myrtle. You usually do."

Well, I was all set to jot you a line the other night, Bernice. I had plainly told myself that just as soon as I got home from work and fixed a bite of supper, that I'd write you a letter. But did I get to? No. Instead, Barney asked me and our grandboy, Buddy, if we'd do him a little favor.

"What kind of little favor do you want us to do, Barney, darlin'?" I asked.

"I'd like you to run over to town for me and pick up a little lumber," he told us.

"Okay. Buddy can drive your truck. I can't see how to drive it at night what with the tinted windows and all," I said.

"Oh, you won't need to take my truck. Take the van. It'll fit in okay. Just slide it under the seats."

So, he gave a list to Buddy and off we went never dreamin' what was before us. Bernice, that man of mine had sent us for fourteen pieces of lumber each one exactly twelve feet long expectin' us to haul it home in a van! We went in and paid for the order and drove around back to get it. I noticed that the young man waitin' on us was lookin' around kinda funny like.

"Look at him, Buddy," I said. "He thinks we've got a flat bed truck settin' in this lumber yard."

"You wasn't plannin' on cartin' it home in that, was you?" he said, pointin' to the van.

"We wasn't, but my husband of forty five years said it'd be no problem," I replied. I just hate it when Barney says that almost as bad as when he's givin' me directions somewhere and says, "You can't miss it."

Anyways, where was I? Oh, yes, in the lumber yard. Well, we found out right quick that there's a metal bar under the van seats that allowed only two boards to slide under and that's with four or five feet danglin' out in mid air! There we was with enough lumber to start a house and nowhere to put it.

"Let's see if we can't let it rest across the seats, Mawmaw," Buddy said, tryin' to calm me down. "I think we can." He thinks the sun rises and sets in his grandpa and was doin' his best to prove we didn't have a problem.

But we had enough of a problem that the young man helpin' us stopped dead in his tracks and said, "Ya'll have to tie it down. I can't be responsible for it."

Buddy thought the young man was scared we'd spill lumber out on the road.

I told Buddy, "He means he ain't gonna take responsibility when them boards hit us in the back of the head and kills us deader than a doornail."

"Don't worry, we can do this, Mawmaw," Buddy said, as he commenced to stretchin' bungee cords everwhere.

When we pulled outta that lumber yard, I felt like I was sittin' on a keg of dynamite. I ask Buddy to drive slow and he did. In fact, he was drivin' so slow that a tractor trailer got right on our rear end and might near gave us a push. Buddy handled that by turnin' up the music's volume on the radio and hollered, "If them boards hit us in the head, I want it put on my tombstone that I died tryin' to please my grandpa Barney."

"Not me," I yelled, tryin' to be heard above Garth Brooks, "If them boards hit me in the back of my head, I want it put on my tombstone that I died because of Barney!"

Well, finally the big truck passed us and we got home safe and sound with the lumber. Barney could tell that I was slightly aggravated when I walked in. He don't see me that way too often and when he does, he takes notice pretty quick.

"Wonder Boy and Wonder Woman have returned," I announced.

"What's the matter? Was there a problem?" he asked.

"Oh, no. It was a piece of cake. But next time, remind us to take helmets, will you?"

Bernice, have you been gettin' along okay? I would love to see you, honey. Do try to come up before the snow flies.

Love,
Myrtle, your friend forever

A Real Snowfall

Dear Bernice,

Did I write and tell you about the big snow we got last year? I mean, I love snow, as you well know, but Bernice, honey, I'm here to tell you that snow was a tad deeper than I like.

Let me tell you about it. In the first place, it arrived on my birthday which was special, I thought. The flakes was beautiful. Big enough that they looked like chunks of tissue paper fallin' on us!

I was tickled with it until it kept on and on snowin'. Our power went out and I stayed home from work one day, which was nice. But, the next day, I felt it my wifely duty to go to work with Barney, bein's the lights was back on and all.

I hurried and got ready to leave for work when Barney did 'cause I knew it would be hard for me to walk down to the store by myself.(The snow was so deep Barney couldn't even get the truck up to the house the night before).

Anyways, where was I? Oh, yes, walkin' down the hill to the store. Barney was in front of me, and I said, "I'll just walk in your tracks, Barney darlin'. That'll make it easier on me."

Wrong. I never knew that Barney took such big steps. Bernice, honey, it was all I could do to step from one of his tracks to the next one.

"Hold up, Barney, darlin'," I shouted. "There ain't no need to rush. We're the only ones crazy enough to be out in this weather. It's not like there'll be a line waitin' for us to open the store." But, did he slow down? NO.

About then, as I was tryin' to pull my foot up and out of his track and into the next 'un, I was kinda like doin' the split and lost my balance and went down in that deep snow! He just kept a goin' like our life depended on us gettin' there on time!

"Will you slow down a bloomin' minute and help me up?" I hollered.

He turned around and said, "My Lord, Myrtle, what are you doin' down there?"

"What does it look like I'm doin', Barney, makin' snow angels?" Did you notice I didn't call him darlin'?

He got hold of my hand and started pullin' me up but all's I could do was waller around in the snow. I was settin' on my leg and couldn't get my bearins. He was about to pull my arm out of its socket when I screamed, "Wait. Turn loose of me. I can do this better by myself." But, I couldn't, Bernice. When I tried to put my hands down on the ground to help myself push up, I was up over my shoulders in snow and my face was half covered. That's how deep the snow was!!

"Lord have mercy, Myrtle, if you ain't in a fix now," Barney said.

"Well, if you'd a took smaller steps, this wouldn't a happened. I can't believe we're goin' to work in this weather anyways. I think your brain has froze up on you, Barney Bridges."

"Calm down, Myrtle," he said, as he tried not to laugh. He tried once more to pull me up and almost fell too.

"Myrtle, don't drag me down with you," he hollered.

By then, we was both laughin' and finally, he got me on my feet. I was covered with snow.

I didn't figure anybody saw us since most people was indoors where they belonged. But, Wanda, next door, bless her heart, told me later that she was lookin' out her window and seen it all.

"I saw you go down, Myrtle. Thought you'd never get up."

"Was you laughin', Wanda?" I asked.

"No, I was too afraid you'd broke your leg."

Now, ain't that sweet? I just love Wanda. But, I'm sure thankful she didn't call 911 and say, "Myrtle's fallen and can't get up."

Bernice, if you get bored with the Florida sunshine and balmy breezes, come on up, honey. I'd say we'll be gettin' some snow before long. We'll build us a snowman.

Send me one of them dinky cards of yours with the palm trees and flamingos waltzin' around under 'em.

Love,
Myrtle, your friend forever

Off to See the Queen

Hello Cora,

My, but it was good to talk to you on the phone last week and hear about another one of your many trips. I told Barney that I'd sure like to take a trip somewhere. Not to stay for long, mind you, but just to get away for a while. Guess what he said? Wait. I'll have to tell you 'cause there ain't no way you'd guess. I still can't believe it myself.

He said, "Myrtle, how would you like to take a trip, say to England?"

Well, Cora, I almost fainted. We've never traveled much and since we moved to the mountains, we've been tied down more than ever, so I wasn't expectin' such a question. Much less one about goin' to England. I've always wanted to meet Queen Elizabeth and her family, so I said, "Barney, darlin', I'd love to go to England, but how will we get there?"

"I reckon we'll fly, Myrtle," he answered. Cora, I'm so excited. This won't be my first flyin' experience but it will be my first time to cross the Atlantic Ocean.

Then, there's another thing. I just saw that movie the other night where a plane was hijacked. Did you see it? The hijackers made the flight attendant sing to 'em. Mercy, I can't get that movie off my mind. At least, I'll know what to sing if our plane is hijacked and they want a singer bein's I was forewarned. Barney keeps tellin' me to forget the movie and my singin' lessons but that's easy for him to say. In the movie, they picked a woman to sing and I just know, in my heart, that I might be the one picked to sing if we're hijacked. I have to be ready for any emergency that might arise, don't you think, Cora, honey?

We're goin' with our son, B.J. and his wife Dil (that stands for daughter-in-law). They've done lots of travelin' but ain't been to England so we'll have a good time, I know. Soon as we get back, I'll write and tell you all about it. If you don't hear from me, watch the news. I might be on it. Well, I'd better close for now and practice my singin' some more.

My first selection will be, "Let There be Peace On Earth" followed by "He's Got The Whole World In His Hands." I like both of them songs and I figure the hijackers will too. And maybe, they'll get the message and turn *their* lives around as well as our plane!

I must close for now.

Love, Myrtle

Castle Fever

Dear Cora,

I bet you just about dropped your teeth when you seen the postmark on this letter, didn't you?

That's right, I'm in Scotland! Even got a picture of me and B.J. standin' in front of a "Welcome To Scotland" sign.

Cora, it's wonderful over here. The beauty of the places of worship is awesome. I've been in small chapels and in cathedrals. It's always the same—angels, rose buds and lacy lookin' beams and columns that look like cake icin'! How them people of long ago could make concrete look like that, I'll never know.

At least, we've switched from castles to churches so I'm not climbin' nearly as many steps as before.

One mornin' B.J. pulled into the parkin' lot of one of them castles and said, "This one's different, Mama. You're gonna love it."

"Where is it, B.J.?" I asked. I couldn't see it from the car.

"It's way over yonder. We can't see it from here but it's one of the best yet," he answered.

"B.J., honey, I'm sittin' this one out. Ya'll run along and take your time," I told 'em.

"You can't do that, Mama. The book says this castle is a must to see while in Scotland. You can't sit in the car while we get to see it. That wouldn't be right," he argued. I knew right then that B.J. was sufferin' from "castle fever."

"And I bet the book says it contains 4,000 steps too. Listen up. I've climbed my last castle step unless I was to come back over here at a later date. I might reconsider if that was to happen. Now, run along, sweetheart. Your mama knows what's she's doin'. Besides, I need to write a few letters," I told him.

Barney piped up about then and said, "I can't let you stay here alone, Myrtle. I'll set here with you, although I do hate to miss this chance to see another castle."

He wasn't foolin' me none. He had "castled" out too. I figured he had a pastry stashed away and planned to devour it while B.J. and Dil was gone. I was right.

When B.J. got back, he reported that we should have gone with 'em. This castle was different. One could see the sea from it, and the color of the stone was reddish. I pictured it, in my mind, and it was lovely. But I had made the right choice, I figured.

Oh, well. I'd better stop this writin' and get ready to see some new sights. We'll head back to London tomorrow to spend a few days before we come home.

Take care and cheerio.

Love,
Myrtle

Mystery Stones

Dear Bernice,

I bet you've been waitin' to hear from me and anxious to know all about Stonehenge. Well, Bernice, I hate to tell you this, honey, but I don't know any more about Stonehenge today than I did when I got off the plane!

But I don't feel so bad. There ain't nobody over here that can tell me what it is. I don't want to confuse you so I'll take you back to when we got there.

We kept seein' the sign and I was so excited 'cause I had heard that everybody goes to Stonehenge when they come to England. Even

B.J. was excited to be goin'. Well, when we parked and got outta the car, the wind was blowin' so hard I had trouble standin' up. It was colder than blue blazes, too. But that's okay, 'cause I can't always brag about our mountain weather. Only I stopped to button up my raincoat and, low and behold, a woman come flyin' by and laid down on the horn and might near scared me to death. It seems that I was in the middle of the road! I thought I was in the parkin' lot. You'd have to be here with me to understand that, I know, but it wasn't laid out the way our roads and parkin' lots are, and I thought I was safe as could be until Miss Horn Blower whizzed by.

Anyways, I caught up with Barney and held on to him so the wind couldn't sweep me away. Then, we paid to go through a gate and followed a path to a circle of rocks! Don't go back to read it again. It was a circle of rocks! They was huge. Some of 'em was the biggest rocks I ever saw -- more like boulders. Some was side by side and had one plopped on top of 'em. Them rocks looked like they was posing for pictures. There they set out in the middle of nowhere. Since they can't talk, nobody knows where they come from, who brought 'em, or why. Ain't that the saddest thing you ever heard?

I don't reckon even the queen knows who put 'em there. But, it put one big question mark in my mind. I had hoped I could figure it all out before I left, but it was so cold, frankly, I didn't give a hoot who put 'em there or why. That's somethin' these people will have to figure out on their own. I will say this: Stonehenge is one of the largest and most important prehistoric monuments in Europe. I just read that in my tourist book. It's a shame they don't know what it means. And another thing, how do they know it's important? When we started turnin' purple, B.J. said, "I hate to rush you, Mama, but if we don't go now, I'll take a chill and won't be able to drive." I beat him back to the car.

I'm in southern England, but nobody has a southern accent over here. It beats all I ever heard. We speak the same language, but it don't come out the same! Which reminds me, if you ever come over here, Bernice, honey, remember to bring some toilet paper with you. I wish somebody had warned me they make theirs outta waxed paper. I must hurry. The "tour guides" are honkin' the horn. I think we're goin' to Wales, the homeland of Tom Jones. Do you remember how I love to hear him sing "Green Grass of Home"?

Cheerio,

Your friend forever,
Myrtle

With One Eye Shut

Dear Cora,

I knew you'd be worryin' about me so I'm goin' to write you real fast like to tell you we got to England safe and sound!

There wasn't no hijackers on our plane, thank goodness. I did get a little nervous once, though, when a strange man looked at me, and I thought he said, "Do you sing?" But Dil said he said, "Good morning."

So I decided right then to quit worryin' about hijackers. But I did ask the Lord to keep watch over us. And it's a good thing I did 'cause when we got off the plane in London and went in the airport low and behold, there was men with guns watchin' for somebody that had threatened to kill some man that had wrote a book that made people real mad in another country.

"Why in the world do they think the man that wrote the book would be here, Barney?" I asked. And get this, Cora. Barney said, "Cause he's hidin' out in London, Myrtle!"

Well, Cora, I got snappy then, and said, "Barney, you sure picked some time for us to come to England, didn't you? You had 37 years to decide to bring me here on vacation and what's gonna happen? I'll tell you what's gonna happen, Barney. We'll get caught up in the middle of a shoot-out in front of Buckingham Palace, that's what!"

"Get control of yourself, Myrtle," he said, "besides, we're rentin' a car and goin' to Wales and Scotland first so maybe all the excitement will be over by the time we get back to London."

Wrong. The excitement come when B.J. got behind the wheel of that rental car! Cora, did you know that they drive on the wrong side of the road over here? It's bad enough to drive in a different car anyways, but to drive on the wrong side of the road in a country where you've never been can be a problem. Dil thought she had a good idea when she said, "B.J., dear, why don't you drive around the parkin' lot and get the feel of the car before we take it out on the road?"

Cora, we could've drove around ever parkin' lot in London and we'd still not be prepared for what I've got a feelin' lies ahead. I may be seein' the sights with one eye shut.

Well, my "tour guides" are in the car waitin' for me to finish this letter and they don't look too happy so I must stop for now. But I told 'em, "Get used to it. I intend to write my friends and keep 'em posted on this vacation. They might be outta sight but they ain't outta mind."

I don't think they understand me, but then, they don't know how I feel about my friends, do they?

Mercy, B.J. has started up the engine. I must go. Remember to pray that he'll be able to "go with the flow," so to speak, and Barney won't have to drive.

Love,
Myrtle

A Wild Ride

Dear Bernice,

What excitement. I feel like I've been on a shootin' star for the past week and I've loved ever minute of it! I decided that I couldn't worry about fast drivin' on the wrong side of the road or I'd not enjoy this vacation.

Just to prove my point, let me tell you what happened the other night. We was runnin' behind schedule gettin' to the bed and breakfast and on top of that, it was cold and rainin' just enough to make drivin' a tad dangerous.

I knew B.J. was drivin' fast, but cars was passin' us like we was standin' still so I was enjoyin' the ride and was cozy as a bug in a rug. About then, Barney whispered, "Myrtle, do you have any idea how fast we're goin'? How can you sit there like you're totally relaxed?"

"I am, Barney. Ain't you ever heard the sayin' before that 'God is my co-pilot'?" I answered.

"He might be your co-pilot, but I'm gonna be your driver before we head back to London. I'm rentin' a car and drivin' us back. I refuse to travel 100 miles an hour under these conditions."

"Barney, darlin', I love you to pieces, but honey, I ain't gettin' in a car if you're gonna be behind the wheel. I just learned how to relax with B.J.'s drivin' and I don't plan to start all over with yours. Not here."

Lord have mercy, there I was with a big problem, I thought. But he changed his mind and continued to ride and drive from the back seat. I'd say his prayer time grew too.

I thought I had been subjected to all the excitement possible in that car. Wrong. Bernice, never in all my life have I ever took such a ride as yesterday when B.J. drove our car into London and returned it to the rental place. It was about 5:00 p.m. and we wasn't sure of where we was suppose to go in the first place. The traffic was whizzin' by on the wrong side of the street, of course. And if a car or taxi wants to pass and ain't got room to do it, that don't matter one bit 'cause they'll run up on the sidewalk and go right on like that's the way one is supposed to drive!! Don't that beat all?

I know that car had to have sides that sucked in or we'd been a goner once or twice. These dear people are nice and have been kind to us when they're standin' on their feet, but when they're in a car, look out!

A foot doctor will have to uncurl my toes. I just know it. We'll be doin' lots of walkin' in London so maybe I can work the curl out of 'em tomorrow by myself.

Our hotel is right by Hyde Park and guess what? There's a place called "Speakers' Corner" and people can go there and speak out on any subject they choose and people stop to hear what they have to say. But I told Barney not to worry. I won't do anything like that. That is, unless I think of something of utter importance and feel directed to speak out. Anyways, we leave on Sunday and that's the day most people do their speakin'. I bet Barney said, "Thank you, Lord, for yet another blessin'."

The man that wrote the book and made them people mad is still hidin' out here so I don't know what will happen. But I ain't gonna worry about that. I'm gonna enjoy seein' the sights with Barney. We may not pass this way again.

Tomorrow, we're gonna ride on a double-decker bus. They scoot all over the city and look like fun. The trains shoot under ground like bullets and get you where you want to go in a flash!

I wish you and Hunter was here, Bernice, to share all this excitement with us. We're goin' to Buckingham Palace. That's where the Queen lives when she's in town. But, I guess you knew that. Anyways, if she's not in town, and I don't get to see her in person, we'll still get to see the Changin' of the Guard. Now, I know she don't exactly receive visitors, but I'd love to see her peek out the window. The people over here love her to pieces.

Speakin' of love, I send mine to you and Hunter. I must stop for now. Tomorrow will be a busy day for me.

Love,
Myrtle, your friend forever

one Last Ride

Dear Bernice,

I know you didn't expect to get another letter from me with a London postmark but I'm so wound up that I can't sleep so I figured I'd write to my forever friend one more time and mail it in the mornin' on our way to the airport.

Bernice, you ain't gonna believe what happened to me and Barney tonight. He wanted us to take one last bus ride around London and I thought that was sweet and kind of romantic 'cause everything looks different at night—all lit up and all and he holds my hand just like he did when we was sweethearts. Well, we still are, but you know what I mean.

Anyways, we got on the bus that we had been on several times thinkin' it would come back to the same spot near our hotel. Wrong! Bernice, honey, we didn't know it but that was the last bus to run that route tonight and it didn't come back into downtown London.

I knew we was in for more excitement when I looked out the window and what did I see? Nothing I had ever seen before. In fact, we was in a rather slummy part of town, if you know what I mean! Not much traffic and no people to speak of.

"Barney, darlin'," I said, "we're in new territory. I can't see Big Ben. I can't see Buckingham Palace. Barney, I can't see London! Just where are we, Barney? We're lost, ain't we?"

"How would I know where we are, Myrtle? I don't live here," he answered. "The driver knows exactly where we are. We're not lost."

"Then, go ask him what we're doin' out here in the boon docks?" I snapped. "Frankly, Barney, I don't like the looks of this neighborhood. I bet the Queen wouldn't be caught dead in it," I practically hollered. "What if that man's hidin' out around here somewhere?"

"What man, Myrtle?" he asked. "You know perfectly well what man. The one that wrote that book, of course. I bet he's in one of them dark buildin's. I knew it. We're never gonna get back home alive. I can see the *Watauga Democrat* headlines now, 'Local couple gunned down outside of London.'"

"Myrtle," Barney said, "just take it easy and calm down. We ain't gonna be in a gun battle. We ain't gonna make headlines in the paper at home." Then he walked up to the driver to ask where we was and was told that we needed to get off that bus and catch another one goin' in the opposite direction. But, listen to this, Bernice. He said we must hurry 'cause the buses stopped runnin' soon and we'd have to catch the train back to London!

So, here we go just like we lived here and knew what we was doin' but we didn't know "beans" about our location. But I could tell from the looks of it that I didn't want to be there in the day much less at night! It was down right spooky.

Speakin' of beans, I can't wait to eat some pinto beans and cornbread. All these people eat is them little green peas that roll around all over your plate. But they catch 'em and smash 'em with their fork and don't have trouble at all. Anyways, I'm surprised they don't have green jaundice over here.

Where was I? Oh, yes, gettin' off the first bus and scootin' to catch the second bus. Well, we got to the bus stop where a man was waitin'. He said he'd been there a long time but none of the buses would stop for him and he had been flaggin' 'em down each and every time.

"The next bus that comes along will stop for us 'cause I'm gonna flag it down and it'll stop or run over me, one or the other," I told him. I'd made my mind up that I'd druther be run over by a bus than shot or taken hostage! And that's exactly what I did too. I figured surely the driver wouldn't let a woman stay out there in the dark. Anyways, the next bus stopped and we rode it to the nearest train station and caught the train back into London. Lord, Bernice, I felt like I was home when the bright lights of London hit my eyes. Oh, it was wonderful. Barney was so calm like he was use to such adventure.

"Barney Bridges," I said, "you're the bravest man I know. Thank you for gettin' me back to the hotel safe and sound." He just gave me one on them grins and said, "No problem."

Surely to goodness my excitement is over for now and in the mornin' we'll head for home. It's been fun, Bernice, but I'm ready to go home and hear some southern accents. I'll write you when I get there. I've packed and now I must get some sleep 'cause I don't sleep too good in the air. I'll fall asleep but then wake up and think about bein' over the ocean and for some reason, I get wide awake. Barney says it's fear. But I told him it ain't fear. If it was, I would never have got on the plane in the first place. I don't have much choice now but I did when I got on the plane in Miami so I know it's not fear, it's excitement and I can't take much more of it.

Cheerio for now.

Love, Myrtle,
Your friend forever

An Excitin' Departure

Bernice, Bernice!

I can't wait till I get home to write and tell you what happened in Heathrow Airport a few hours ago so while everybody's snoozin', I'll write to you right fast like. I can't sleep over the ocean anyways.

I know I'm all the time tellin' you "you ain't gonna believe this" but this time, you really ain't gonna believe this, Bernice. But I'll swear on our friendship that it's the truth.

Let me start at the beginnin'. We took a cab from the hotel to Heathrow Airport and it was rainin' just a tad so I had on my raincoat. That seemed like the most likely thing to have on, don't you think? I didn't figure I'd look like a dangerous woman.

Well, picture us in that busy airport with all kinds of people from all over the world just waitin' for a terrorist to cut loose with a gun or bomb or whatever they cut loose with. When we started through customs (this is what you ain't gonna believe) this woman security person said out loud for all to hear, "Step over here, Madam."

I looked to see who she was talkin' to and discovered she was talkin' to me! Well, I looked at Barney and he looked like he was about to lose his best friend.

"What does she want, Barney?" I whispered.

"Do what she says, Myrtle."

"Madam, over here, please," she said again. "I need to search you for security reasons." Bernice, do I look like a terrorist to you? I think not. Anyways, I walked over to her and she got very personal, if you know what I mean.

"Lady," I said. "I don't know what on earth you're lookin' for, but I'd bet my passport you ain't gonna find it. You might try checkin' out that man over yonder wearin' the purple turban. He looks suspicious, don't you think? Or the one in that black leather jacket with the patch over his left eye. All's I've got on me is a box of Correctol, my passport, writin' paper and a pen. I sure bud can't hijack a plane with that," I told her. "I wouldn't pluck a bird's feather, for goodness sake."

"Does the Queen know about this? Get her on the phone," I said. By now, Barney had set down and was readin' a paper. I don't know why he was readin' the paper 'cause he already knew the news. That writer feller was still hidin' out in London. He was makin' the headlines everyday.

"Lady, while I have been in your fair country, I have looked down gun barrels and have been lookin' over my shoulder the whole time expectin' somebody to grab me. Rest assured you don't have to worry about me causin' you trouble. Mercy, I love your country."

The woman security person searched till she knew I wasn't a threat to the British government and then invited me to come back for another visit sometime. Here I had worried all week that a terrorist was gonna put a hurtin' on London, and they had the audacity to suspect me! Well, I never. I might write the Queen a letter when I get home. She needs to know about this, don't you agree?

I might have picked up a slight British accent, I don't know. Wouldn't care if I did. It's so perky. But then, come to think of it, "ya'll" is gonna sound like music to my ears when I get home.

I must close my final vacation letter high above the Atlantic Ocean. I hope you enjoyed comin' along with me via the mail.

Much love,
Myrtle, your friend forever

off to Scandinavia

Cora, honey,

Guess what? Time's up 'cause you won't guess anyways. I'm gonna tell you somethin' that I can't believe myself. I mean, I keep pinchin' myself to make sure I ain't dreamin'. Cora, are you settin' down?

You remember how me and Barney went to Great Britain last year, don't you, and how I wrote all them letters tellin' about it? Well, get ready, Cora, here comes my news. Barney's takin' me to Scandinavia!! I told you you wouldn't believe it. That's a far cry from goin' down the mountain to Wal-Mart, ain't it?

He was calm as could be the other day (ain't he always?) when he said, "Myrtle, how would you like to go to Scandinavia?" That's them countries that are kinda bunched together off to the side of where we went last time, I think.

"Are B.J. and Dil takin' another trip, Barney?" I asked. We went with them last time remember?

"No, it'll just be us this time," he answered, and he had that cute little grin on his face.

"How romantic, Barney, darlin'. I'd love to go, but how can we be away from the store for so long?" I asked.

He said that we won't live forever and we need to enjoy life more and takin' another trip will be good for us and he's got it all figured out and he's asked a friend to help Camille run the store. Don't that sound simple enough?

Have you and Homer ever been to Scandinavia? I can't remember you tellin' me if you have. I'm sure you would of, too.

Mercy, I've got so much to do. I wish I had time to learn the languages that's spoke over there, but Barney said there wasn't enough time left in the world for me to do that! Anyways, they spoke English in Great Britain and half the time, I couldn't understand what was bein' said. But that's okay; I don't think they could understand me half the time either.

Well, enough of this jibber jabber. I've got lots to do. Watch for my letters from across the Atlantic and pray for our safety, please. There's lots goin' on over there right now. I heard somethin' about the Berlin Wall comin' down but it's not in Scandinavia so I reckon we'll get to enjoy a calmer vacation this time. Do you know whatever happened to that man that wrote that book that made so many people mad? Remember how he was hidin' out in London when we was there? I just knew that we'd get caught in the middle of a shoot-out in front of Buckingham Palace. Lord, I do hope he didn't go to Copenhagen! Oops, there I go to worryin' and Barney wants me completely relaxed and worry-free this trip, bless his heart.

Don't answer this letter 'cause I won't be home. Call Bernice and tell her all my news and tell her I'll be writin' from far, far away again. Thanks a bushel.

Much love to you and Homer.

Your friend forever,
Myrtle

Where are the Hijackers?

Dear Bernice,

I hope Cora called to tell you that me and Barney are "on the go" again. I promised I'd write my friends and family so's they could feel like they was goin' right along with me. And what do you know? You're gettin' my first letter.

Lucky for me, Barney is pooped out right now and is restin' in the hotel lobby while we're waitin' for our room to be tidied up. He didn't sleep too good on the way over, and it's a good thing 'cause if he wasn't tired, he'd be out walkin' around seein' the sights of Copenhagen, Denmark and I couldn't be writin' you.

He saw me gettin' my pad and pen out and said, "Don't tell me you're about to write Bernice already. You just got here."

"Okay, Barney, I won't tell you. But would you druther I call her to tell her we got here safe and sound?" I asked.

"No, no. Go right ahead and write her a nice long letter. Whatever makes you happy," he mumbled.

"My happiness ain't important here, Barney," I said. "What's important is that my friend will know I'm thinkin' about her and **that** will make her happy, bless her heart."

So, let's see. First, let me tell you about the plane ride, Bernice. I was utterly amazed at the movie screen we could watch and see a map of exactly where our plane was, how fast it was flyin', the air temperature and the amount of time since our departure from Chicago! Don't that beat all? At one point, I woke Barney up to tell him what I thought was some breakin' news, so to speak, like they do on TV when shockin' things happen.

"Don't act like you know this, Barney, darlin', and don't get scared. We have to be brave for the other passengers. Evidently, they ain't as alert as me. Look at the map now. We ain't flyin' across the Atlantic no more, Barney. Only the Lord and the hijackers know where we're headed," I whispered.

"What hijackers?" he practically yelled. Bless his heart, he had been in a dead sleep.

"*Ssshhh,*" I quietly tried to comfort him and pointed out that our plane was no longer goin' across the Atlantic toward Scandinavia but was way north over the tip of Greenland! "It's as plain as the map in front of us, Barney. Our pilot is no longer in control of this plane!"

"You watched that movie again, didn't you, Myrtle?"

"What movie?"

" You know what movie. The one where that plane gets hijacked."

"No, but would you look at our flight attendant. Have you ever laid eyes on such a brave young woman?" I asked. "Who would think from her actions that this plane is bein' commandeered by hijackers? Bless her brave heart, while under such horrible pressure, she's tryin' her best to make us think that everything's hunky-dory, ain't she, Barney? She's just a fluffing' pillows and smilin'."

"That's because everything is hunky-dory, Myrtle. The only pressure she's under is cabin pressure. Now, go to sleep."

"Surely you jest. How do you expect me to sleep when I'm bein' took by force to a destination known only to the pilot and the hijackers. Honestly, Barney, you are the calmest man I know! Get a life."

"If you know so much, Myrtle, where are the hijackers?" he asked. "Point 'em out to me." He was wide awake now and a little wild eyed.

"I will. I'm goin' to the bathroom now and I'll look for 'em. I bet they're behind that curtain up yonder," I told him. Lucky for us, they wasn't and before long, the map showed we was droppin' down towards Great Britain and then over towards Denmark.

"I hope you're happy. I was wrong. You was right," I told Barney. "And you better believe this, buddy boy. On the way home, if we're hijacked, I won't wake you up to tell you."

"Is that a promise, Myrtle?" he asked.

Oh, I almost forgot. Bernice, remember them raspberry frosties we use to get at the 7-11 store? Well, when daylight come and we looked out the window, our plane was above the clouds and Bernice, I kid you not, it looked like we had a big raspberry frosty under us. It was a beautiful blessin', Bernice.

Just think, if you had been on that plane with me, we could of talked for hours and hours nonstop. Oh, what a wonderful thought.

Well, it looks like our room is ready so I'll close for now. But I'll be writin' you again real soon.

Much love from your friend forever,
Myrtle

Smoke Angel

Greetin's from Norway, Bernice.

I wanted to write and tell you about our day in Oslo, Norway while it's still fresh in my mind. We have to wait about one hour before we can get on the boat goin' back to Denmark so I told Barney, "I think I'll use this time to write to Bernice." Then, I added, "Or I could call her, Barney."

With that, he said, "Don't let me bother you, Myrtle, honey. You sit right there and write Bernice and I'll ramble around a bit while we wait."

Oslo was real nice, Bernice, and we took a tour bus and saw lots of interestin' places. But I don't have time to write about it all now. I'll do that later.

Bernice, I'm sittin' here lookin' at a man that's waitin' to get on our boat and he don't look like your basic traveler, if you know what I mean. For one thing, he don't have a suitcase with him. Bernice, he's carryin' a paper bag!

I think I'll mosey over by where he's sittin' and see if I can tell what's in that bag. He might be the very person that set fire to that other boat and how do I know that he don't plan to do the same thing on our boat?

Mercy, I feel like Colombo or whoever that detective was that wore the rain coat all the time and played it so cool. Remember? Where is Barney when I need him? Well, I don't really need him 'cause he'd just say, "Myrtle, you're lettin' your imagination run wild again."

I ain't lived with him all these years without learnin' what he's gonna say before he says it. But since I don't want to be treadin' water tonight, I'm takin' matters in my own hands and I'm gonna know the whereabouts of that man, if I can, and what's in that bag, when we get on the boat.

Bernice, if we get back to Copenhagen safe and sound in the mornin', and I pray that we will, we'll be goin' straight to the train station to go to Berlin. I've asked the Lord to send one of His angels with us and I know He will. Come to think of it, I'd better ask Him to put one on our boat tonight too. One that can sniff out smoke real good. I'll write you again, soon as I can.

Love,
Myrtle, your friend forever

Self-Appointed Fire Marshal

Bernice, Bernice!

I just got back from reservin' our table for supper, I mean dinner. Anyways, guess who was sittin' in the lobby two decks up? You won't guess so I'll tell you. It was that man, Bernice. The one with the paper bag and no luggage. Remember?

The bag was sittin' on the floor by his feet and it was partly opened! He was sound asleep. I felt it my duty to the captain and crew and all the passengers to look in that bag and mercy, Bernice, I wish I hadn't! That bag contained a roll of toilet paper!! Do you know how fast toilet paper burns? Does excitement follow me or what?

Well, I come barrelin' back to Barney and tried to be the calm person he is but I felt like a news reporter with breakin' news. One that had just hit on somethin' big, if you know what I mean. But do you think Barney got excited? Nooo.

When I told him the bag had toilet paper in it, he said, "Maybe the poor guy's got diarrhea, Myrtle. Did you think of that? Did you spot a book of matches, too, in the middle of all your nosiness?"

"No, I didn't, and I'm not nosey, Barney. Well, not much anyways, and I didn't see no matches. I was afraid he'd wake up and find me standin' over him. I didn't have time for a proper inspection. Besides, seein' the paper was enough to send me runnin' back to warn you with chills up my spine."

Bernice, Barney should be proud of me, don't you think? I told him I bet there's not another woman on this boat like me, brave enough to take matters in her own hands.

Barney said, "I know for a fact there ain't another woman on this boat like you, Myrtle. And for all the men on this boat, I'm ever so thankful for that."

You know, Bernice, if and when I get back home, I might just volunteer my services down at the Volunteer Fire Department. I'm sure they could use more help, don't you think? 'Specially in the line of investigation.

Well, Barney says he's hungry as a bear so I must hurry.

I don't see how he can be hungry with danger lurkin' all around us, do you? I tell you, Bernice, the man has no fear. I sure know how to pick 'em, don't I? I'm gonna eat light tonight because they say one shouldn't take to the water with a full stomach. I've got to study the fire instructions real good before I go to bed. I probably won't be able to sleep so I might write you again after Barney drops off to sleep and tell you about supper, I mean dinner. Sure would love to have some corn bread and soup beans but it'll never happen.

Oh, well, gotta go.

Love,
Myrtle, your friend forever.

Kirsten and Peter

Dear Claudine,

You should be on this train with me and Barney. We are having a time talkin'. Not to each other so much but to the couple that's in our little compartment with us. They both speak English. Oh, it's wonderful to communicate again.

The woman's name is Kirsten. When she says it, her voice kinda roller coasters, if you know what I mean. Oh, she 's cute as can be. She's got blondish hair and blue eyes and she's a school teacher. She's from Denmark, but get this. She teaches German to children in Denmark. She's on her way to a weddin' in East Germany.

Now the man, his name is Peter. He's on his way to West Berlin to some kind of art festival that his friend's in. He says he's an artist, too, but I wonder, bless his heart. I'm afraid he's got a problem. He keeps jumpin' up to get a drink of something he's carryin' in a bottle in his suitcase. I will say this for him though. He's polite. He ain't missed a time yet offerin' me and Barney a drink! I lost track about the tenth time. Not because my mind wasn't clear, mind you. I've not accepted anything and neither has Barney.

Claudine, we tried to get Peter to go eat with us in the cafeteria while we was on the ferry but he wouldn't. That's why I think he's got a problem.

Kirsten went with us though. She ate some kind of soup and bread. That's all she wanted. She said she ain't use to eatin' much.

Guess what I ate? A big servin' of German potato salad! Oh, was it ever good. The best thing I've tasted since I left home.

When we got back to our compartment and settled in once again, Kirsten and Peter started askin' us questions about our life in America. They had already told us that they didn't have a car. They can't afford one.

I felt very humble when they wanted to know if we owned one. I answered, "yes." They wanted to know all about it. We told 'em what kind it was but didn't tell 'em that we had a truck too.

Claudine, I felt guilty to tell 'em about our blessin's back at home. I waited for their questions before I said anything about us. We ought not ever complain about our life in America. We've got so much more than we deserve, you know? They wanted to know how we make our livin' and asked all about our store and did we have problems gettin' supplies. Peter asked if we sold beer, bless his heart.

Kirsten pointed out a big apartment building to us as the train zipped by that don't even have heat in it durin' the winter! Can you believe that? When we pull into the train stations to wait for passengers to get on, it's strange. It's quiet. Too quiet. I don't see smiles on anybody's faces. I think about you and how you smile so sweetly all the time. These people couldn't have much to smile about. Kirsten says it won't be like this in West Berlin. I hope she's right.

She touched my heart when she was tellin' me about the weddin' she's goin' to. "Wait a minute," she said. "Let me show you what I brought to carry to the reception."

I wondered what it was and was surprised when she opened her bag and pulled out a little flag. It was Denmark's flag.

"Won't it be great to wave my flag in the crowd?' she asked.

Claudine, this made me want to cry seein' her enthusiasm and all. Simple pleasures are important to her and should be more important to us.

You know what? When it was time for her to get off this train, I felt like I was sayin' goodbye to a friend. She hugged Barney and Peter and me and turned around and waved to us after she got off the train. I know I'll never see her again. But we're goin' to look for each other in heaven. We talked about that.

It's quiet now that Kirsten's gone. I think I'll put my writin' pad away and rest a spell. Claudine, my poor ankles are swellin'. I guess it's from sittin' so long. Just a few more hours and we'll be gettin' off this train and headed for new adventures.

Much love to you my friend.

Myrtle

Berlin, Heeere's Barney

Dear Hazel,

I bet you didn't expect another letter from me so soon but while I have the chance, I wanted to tell you about the trip from Copenhagen to Berlin.

Thank goodness, Peter, the young man that rode in our compartment understood English and German good. After the ferry reached land in Germany, our car was hooked to another train and off we went through the countryside. We stopped at several stations along the way and picked up passengers. It was on one of these stops that we heard a terrible racket. I couldn't make out a word the people was sayin' but it sounded like somebody was upset!

Peter stepped out of our compartment to find out what was wrong. He come back in and said, "I think they want everybody off the train."

"Not me, they don't," I told him with my voice a little higher and louder than normal, "If I get off this train in East Germany, I'll be kickin' and screamin' so loud they'll need ear plugs. Barney, we ain't gettin' off this train till we get to West Berlin, are we? Okay?"

"Calm down, Myrtle," he said. "Why would they want us off this train? They've checked our passports every single time we've stopped at a station." And they did, Hazel. They'd look at us and then look at our passport picture like they thought we was spies.

About then, Peter went out again and stayed a few minutes. We could hear all this jibber jabber and finally he come back in and said that they were lookin' for someone who shouldn't be on the train. Evidently, they got the person off and, we went on our way. Praise be.

Oh, how thankful I was for Peter. After we got to West Berlin, we stood in the station and talked with him a few minutes. Barney gave him our card and told him to look us up if he ever comes to America.

Then, we got a taxi and it brought us to the hotel. That's where I am now. It's a beautiful hotel, Hazel, almost elegant. It's the only place the ticket agent in Copenhagen could find 'cause so many people are here right now. The train station was runnin' over with people comin' in to celebrate their new freedom with the wall comin' down and all. It's excitin', Hazel. I'm glad Barney was determined to bring me here.

Speakin' of Barney, I don't know where he is right this minute. Can you believe that? When we got to the hotel and walked in this room, I said, "Look at that bed, Barney. I can't wait to get in it."

Guess what he said? I'll tell you 'cause you won't guess.

He said, "Before we take a shower, Myrtle, do you want to take a little walk around West Berlin?"

Hazel, it was 11:00 and pitch dark!

"Barney Bridges, look at my ankles. They're as big as grapefruit. Do they look like they want to take a walk? I'm so tired I feel years beyond my age," I said, and that ain't good. I need my rest. But, if you want to take a walk this late at night in a place you've never been, go right ahead."

He did!

If he stays much longer, I'll have time to write Bernice too. But, I might have to wait 'cause this bed feels wonderful and I'm so tired.

I told Barney to remember he's not at the mall back home. I do hope he gets back to me safe and sound. He's got my passport! I'm sure he will, though. He's got one of them angels I asked for walkin' with him.

Much love to you,
Myrtle

History in the Makin'

Dear Bernice,

Fancy, fancy, fancy. You ain't never seen nothin' like it, I know. I'm talkin' about this hotel. I reckon it's okay if that's what a body likes. But, me? I like less fancy and more friendly, if you know what I mean. I found out that I don't like boats and I ain't crazy about hotels either.

This place could use a lesson in southern hospitality. Everbody's too busy for their own good, if you ask me. I turned on the television last night and when I saw CNN's Bernard Shaw I might near cried! It felt good to hear a clear American accent. They seemed like "family". But, honey, don't get me wrong. I'm havin' a good time, really, even if it don't sound like it.

Just like in Copenhagen, West Berlin's got little mini entertainment shows everwhere you turn. We'll be walkin' along and hear music comin' from down the street or around the corner. It's confusin' but I reckon the entertainers collect enough donations to live on. At least, they're workin' for it. I will say that.

Well, let me tell you what we did today. We took a tour bus ride into East Berlin. The wall's comin' down, but they let only people with special permission pass back and forth, except people on the bus. They're still workin' out the problems before it'll be "business as usual" again. Today was the second day the tour bus was allowed in the east side of Berlin.

Bernice, we saw old buildin's that had been sprayed with bullets! The holes marked the spots just as plain as day. We saw buildin's with windows that had iron welded across 'em. Bernice, people got shot tryin' to get from the east side of Berlin to the other! People tried to jump out of buildin's and was cut down like weeds. Talk about feelin' sick to your stomach. That's how I felt when we saw a spot where little white crosses stood. I was lookin' out on the very spot where people had died tryin' to get to freedom. Mercy, I never had such a day. The East German guards kept gettin' on the bus and lookin' at everbody's passports. I mean they looked us over good.

Have you ever heard of Check Point Charlie? Me and Barney was right there lookin' at it-walkin' around it. They're gonna be tearin' it down before long. It's just a little guard buildin' on the border where people had to pass and be checked out for safety's sake. It's a famous place though. All the war movies had people passin' through there. Remember? Thank the Lord, a more peaceful life has come for these people and it won't be needed anymore.

I can't describe the difference between the two sections of Berlin good enough. It's like two different worlds. Wealth and poverty. Happiness and gloom. Day and night. I'll never forget the difference between the two.

That's enough about sad stuff. Guess what was on television in the little cafe we ate supper, I mean dinner, in tonight? I know for a fact you ain't gonna guess this one so's I'll tell you.

Here sits me and Barney as we enjoy some really good food for a change. We ordered this beef and cabbage dish that was outta this world and enough to feed a family of six. Anyways, the waitress was kind enough to explain what was what and recommended what we ordered. Too bad she didn't tell me we'd never in this world be able to clean our plates. I felt terrible, too. After seein' such sad conditions, I didn't want to waste. But, I had no choice.

Anyways, where was I? Oh, yes. I was tellin' you about the television program. We watched the NASCAR race comin' from Martinsville, Virginia in the U.S. of A! I said, teasin' Barney, "Barney, darlin', I know you love racin' but did you have to come all the way over here to see that race? Couldn't you of watched it at home?"

After we finished eatin', we strolled around town and spotted a great big church. Tomorrow, I hope I can find it again. I want to see it in daylight. Barney says he wants us to walk along the wall and find a section he saw from the train as we come into town. It had a great big hole in it. I don't know if we can locate it or not. But, if I know

Barney, and I do, he'll find what he's lookin' for. He's wantin' a piece of the wall from that spot, I think.

My word, I just noticed the time. It's late and I must get ready for another big day tomorrow and get my rest. I hope you've been well and happy while I've been away. Can't wait to send you some pictures.

Love, your friend forever,
Myrtle

The Long Walk

Dear Cora,

Since I wrote Bernice several letters from here, I'm gonna write to you this time. Well, I might send Bernice a card to keep me from feelin' guilty but it's your turn for a letter.

Barney wonders why I don't run out of things to write about. Cora, I told him that he's my source of writin' inspiration. Mercy, if we didn't have a time today!

This morning we took a cab to the Wall.

"Where do you want to go?" the driver asked.

"Just take us to the Wall. It don't matter where," Barney told him. So the driver zipped us right over to the Berlin Wall.

"Where to now, Barney?" I asked, as I climbed outta the cab.

"Let's go this way with the crowd," he said. "I want to find that section with the big hole in it. The one I spotted from the train on the way in."

Well, we walked and walked and picked up pieces of the wall as we went. A man was knockin' the day lights out of it and sellin' chunks to tourists so Barney bought some of that so's we'd have some of the real thing for sure.

He had the video camera rollin' and we got some real good shots and in the background you can hear all kinds of languages as people talk to each other about the Wall.

Two East German guards was standin' on the other side of the Wall where there was a huge openin' and they saw Barney had a camera. Barney said, "Go over there and stand and see if they'll let me make your picture with 'em."

They tried to look stern until I said, "Do ya'll mind if my husband makes ya'lls picture with me?" For some reason, that made 'em chuckle and they adjusted their hats and posed with me just as pretty as you please. Barney made three and we gave 'em both one. They acted so proud to have their picture made.

Well, we walked some more because Barney was sure we was gettin' close to the spot he wanted to see. Before we knew it, Cora, we was in a strange section of town. It looked like we was in another country —like Turkey!

People looked at us like we was way out of where we should have been, which we was. All the doors was opened and we could look in only nobody had lights on inside.

"Barney, I feel like eyes are on us from inside them places," I told him. "Let's get back to where we know our way around. It'll be dark before we know it."

"We'll be back to familiar sights in a minute," he assured me. But I didn't think so.

"Here comes a man meetin' us," Barney said. "I'll ask for directions."

That was a joke. The man hid his face and wouldn't slow down! He practically ran down the sidewalk away from us.

"Barney Bridges, he thinks you're Hugh Downs and I'm Barbara Walters. He thinks we wanted to interview him for *20/20!*" I yelled.

"Why in the world would he think a thing like that, Myrtle? Loosen up. This is a chance of a lifetime to roam through this community," he told me.

"You'll think 'loosen up' when we're tied up. What it is, is serious business, Barney. We're lost in dangerous territory. This ain't down town West Berlin remember. This section is like another country stuck in Germany or hadn't you noticed? How do you know that somebody ain't gonna jump out and grab us and take us hostage?" I yelled. "Don't you read the paper, Barney? It happens all the time in this world of unrest. And that big camera you're carryin' tells 'em that we don't exactly belong here. It's gettin' dark, Barney," I said. "You can roam all night if you want to, but I'm hailin' the first cab God sends my way." And Cora, that's exactly what I did and believe you me, Barney was right on my heels hoppin' in that cab.

When we got back to the hotel, we was in for a surprise when we watched the movie he made at the Wall. Now, Barney don't lay claim that he's a professional cameraman, mind you. And I don't mean to be puttin' him down but after he got some good shots of the Wall, we walked along side it for quite a ways. He had forgot to turn the camera off. In a way, that's good. Our family and friends can like -

walk with us along the wall and hear what we was sayin' about it. That is, if they can understand us. We was both pantin' like a pack of dogs.

Tonight is our last night here. We'll catch the train tomorrow night and go back to Copenhagen and straight to the airport to head home.

The train station is called "The Berlin Zoo Station" because it's next to the zoo. We're gonna put our luggage in a locker and spend the day at the zoo. I told Barney I wanted to spend our last day there because I'll get to "people watch" some more and will get to observe more of God's creatures big and small. Cora, I'm so happy. This trip has been such a blessin' and such a treat. I'll call you when we get home. Our best to you and Homer.

Love, Myrtle,
your friend forever

A Thoughtful Departure

Dear Bernice,

Well, our short stay in West Berlin is about over. In fact, I'm sittin' on a bench this very minute waitin' for our train to get here. Just watchin' the trains come and go is excitin'. These people know how to provide good service for travelers. It's amazin' to watch the clock and know it's time for a train to pull in and then to hear it comin' smack dab on time! It's got to be on time or else it'll be rammed by the next train! Beats all I've ever seen. But then, I ain't spent much time observin' train station policy in my own country, much less overseas.

I got a little concerned when a train kept sittin' here longer than normal. "Wonder why that train is still here, Barney?" I asked.

"Don't know, Myrtle, but it has been sittin' there longer than the others, hadn't it? That's odd," he said, as he got up to mosey around.

Then, he come back with the news that another train was bringin' passengers that had to connect with the one sittin' here and they was waitin' as long as they could before pullin' out and gettin' out of the way of the next train behind them.

Low and behold, we heard a whistle and here comes a train zoomin' in on my left. It hadn't even come to a complete stop when this couple jumped off of it and ran directly in front of my bench and jumped on the waitin' train and it was gone in a flash and here comes the next train behind it before I could say, "Thank you, Lord."

We had a wonderful day today in the zoo. I don't have time now to tell you about it now because it's time for our train but I promise to do that later.

I do hope we'll have people on the trip back to Copenhagen who can speak English. At least, we'll know what to expect goin' back. We'll be on the train all night and will go directly to the airport and then head home. I bet I can get in a letter or two before mornin', don't you?

Bernice, I hear our train comin' and it's right on time. You know, I feel teary. This city has touched my life and has made me have a feelin' of sadness for people I didn't even know. But I did see the bullet holes that took some of their lives away simply because they couldn't stand it any longer; not havin' their freedom, I mean, and they was willin' to take the chance to escape.

I'm goin' home prouder than ever to be a citizen of the United States and more thankful than ever before for all my blessin's in life. I know I'll never come this way again but I thank the Lord for this one time.

Barney's motionin' for me to get on the train with him. Guess I'd best do that, don't you think?

Much love, your friend forever,
Myrtle

Headin' Home

Dear Claudine,

Me and Barney's makin' our way back home now. What a time we've had! I must hurry with this letter 'cause I don't want the couple that's in this compartment with us to think I'm rude and don't want to talk to them.

They're real nice, Claudine. Her name is Thorna and his is Peter. When we got on the train, I thought we'd be by ourselves since nobody was in here with us. Then, Thorna came in and said something that I couldn't understand.

I smiled and said, "Only English."

She smiled real big and said, "Good, we talk English."

This couple is married and live in Copenhagen. They use to have a car but Peter sold it because they couldn't afford to keep it.

Besides, he don't need it all that much since the transportation system is so good. They take the train when they go anywhere. They've been to Poland on some kind of school band trip and they said conditions are real bad there. Thorna said toilet paper is a prized possession where they were.

Claudine, I never dreamed people do without so much in other parts of the world. We talked last night for a long time about our trip and they asked a million questions about our life in America.

Then, we decided to settle down and try to get some sleep. We cut the light off and tried to get comfy. Well, that didn't last long, the settlin' down part.

Just as I was droppin' off to sleep, Thorna had a nightmare and commenced to screamin' at the top of her lungs! Scared me and Barney half to death.

"Wake up, Thorna," Peter hollered. "You're havin' a bad dream."

She felt bad that she had scared us and told us that she was dreamin' about gettin' caught because they hadn't used the right passport to do their travelin' (they really hadn't). Poor thing was worn out because they had slept on a bench for two nights.

Well, anyways, she was dead tired and we was wide awake thanks to her screamin'. By then, our car had been put on the ferry so Barney, Peter and me went to the cafeteria for a cup of coffee and a sweet roll. That thing musta been made last month. When we got back to Thorna, she was asleep, bless her heart, so we all got a little rest.

We're not far from Copenhagen now and Peter and Thorna said that they'd direct us to the bus at the train station that will take us to the airport.

Claudine, I don't mind to tell you that I am pooped. Pooped, but still excited. Our trip is about over but it will always be alive in my memory.

Well, sweet friend, I will close for now and talk to our new friends while I still have the chance. We'll never see them again and I feel kinda sad about that.

I have just about wore my feet and right hand out on this vacation. It's no wonder, is it?

I'll call you when I get home.

Much love,
Myrtle

The Unfriendly Sky

Dear Hazel,

You could tell from the postmark on this letter that I'm home now. Lawsy mercy, what a vacation me and Barney had! My head's still spinnin' from all the excitement.

Never in all my born days have I experienced such a wonderful time. To tell the truth, it was like a historical honeymoon. You know, romance and a big history lesson all rolled into one.

You know I love Barney to pieces but I did get a tad aggravated at him on the flight from Chicago back to Charlotte. I plainly told him that I intended to sleep on our last leg home. We lost so much sleep on the train back to Copenhagen. Was it you or Claudine that I wrote and told about that? Honey, I wrote so many letters I don't know who I told what.

Anyways, like I said, I just wanted to shut my eyes and meditate for a while and fall asleep. 'Twas not meant to be.

In the first place, this was not a smooth ride. That plane bounced around like a bouncin' ball. Barney was not a happy flier. Me? I was so tired I didn't give a hoot. Just as I got fixed and was almost in dreamland, he pounded on my leg and say, "Are you asleep?"

"I was right on the verge, Barney. What do you want?" I asked.

"This is the roughest ride yet, don't you think? I don't like it, Myrtle. I don't like it at all," he said.

"Go to sleep, Barney. It'll make the time go by faster," I told him.

"I just know we're gonna hit one of them air pockets any minute, Myrtle, and you can kiss me good-bye. My heart can't handle the pressure. How can you sleep at a time like this?" he asked.

"If you'll stop poundin' on my leg long enough, I'll show you," I told him. "That pilot's got everthing under control. He don't need me to stay awake or you either, for that matter."

"How is it you worry about things that don't happen but the very things that are happenin' you don't worry about. I don't get it, Myrtle," he said.

Well, bless his heart, he never did relax so I stayed awake and talked to him all the way to Charlotte. Even I was glad that it was a short flight and it wasn't like that crossin' over the ocean. My legs would never have been in shape for all the walkin' we done.

Hazel, honey, it's your turn to write to me and let me know how you're gettin' along.

I'd better write Bernice a letter now so she'll know I'm home safe and sound.

Love, Myrtle

Goodbye, Erma

Dear Bernice,

I write this letter with a sad heart. You must have read in the paper that Erma Bombeck died. I saw it on the news the other night and might near cried.

Barney said, "She had been real sick. Didn't you know that?"

I knew she had been sick but somehow I thought she'd be all right. She lifted my spirits so much every time I read her column.

Bernice, honey, do you remember how you use to call me if you read her column first to see if I had read it? We never missed readin' it 'cause she understood what it was to be a wife and mother of small children and then, later on, bless us all, the mother of teenagers!

Once we laughed till we cried 'cause we swore she had been in our house listenin' to us talk about Barney and Hunter! Evidently, her husband behaved like them sometimes.

Why I remember once I snuggled up in my afghan, the one my mama made me, and opened up her latest book at the time called "When You Look Like Your Passport Photo, It's Time to Go Home."

This was after me and Barney had been to Great Britain with B.J. and Dil. Anyways, Barney was settin' there readin' the paper. I read a few pages and commenced to smilin'. Before I knew it, I was laughin'. Every chapter got funnier. Finally, I was so slap happy that Barney noticed I was actin' goofy and said," Myrtle, what in the world are you readin?"

I was wipin' tears from my eyes from laughin' so hard but I tried to speak to Barney in a calm manner. He ain't seen me lose control all that much in the many years we've been married. "Barney, darlin', she had to be in the car with us."

"Who had to be in the car with us. Where?" he asked.

"Erma Bombeck," I told him, "when we rented our car in England. She knows exactly how it felt to climb all them castle steps and pray for soft toilet paper and drive in a strange land on the wrong side of the road."

She had been in as many cathedrals as us too. I was impressed by the first dozen or so, like her, but was ready to move on to something different after a while.

She never let her fame go to her head, did she, Bernice? She gave this world, or the people who read her writin's, a real blessin'. I hope I can do that someday, Bernice, if I ever get published. I hope I can cause a smile to break out on some soul's face and tickle their spirit just the way Erma tickled ours.

I do hope you're well and happy. Wish I could see you and could sit a spell with you and have a cup of your good coffee.

Oh well, I'd better stop this daydreamin' and get busy. Just wanted to tell you about Erma in case you didn't know.

Love, Myrtle,
your friend forever

A family feast

Dear Claudine,

What have you got planned for Thanksgivin'?

We'll go down the mountain if it don't snow and gather with my relatives at noontime. We made a promise to Grandma that we'd always, always get together at least once a year after her and Grandpa left this world and that's exactly what we do.

Grandma and Grandpa had a big family (seven girls and lots of grandchildren and great-grandchildren, plus husbands and all) so when we gather, there's a crowd 'cause if possible, everybody comes to this big church that lets us use their fellowship buildin'. Mercy, we've got a gang.

Anyways, one year, Cousin Wade, volunteered to set up the tables and place the food on 'em as it was brought in so's the women would have more time for hugs and kisses.

The ladies was real happy that he wanted to help and said, "It's about time the younger ones took charge of our feast."

Well, to make a long letter short, after we asked the blessin', and was ready to fill our plates, we noticed that the servin' tables wasn't pushed together in a long, organized line. The food was sorta scattered here and there.

Some people went to one table, some to another and everybody was movin' in all directions! We looked like we had never marched down a buffet line before in our life. It went like this:

"Hey, Sparkle, how are you?"

"Just fine, Myrtle, and you?"

"Great. Say, where did you find my macaroni and cheese?"

"Over by the carrot cake."

"Thanks."

"Coral Bell, you're lookin' good."

"You too, Myrtle. Excuse me, but are those Hyacinth's dumplin's?"

"Yep."

"Where in the world did you get 'em?"

"Let's see. I think by the red Jell-O."

"Mimosa, I'm so glad to see you and them turnips. Did my mama bring them?" I asked.

Rose said, "No. Dahlia always brings the kraut salad. Don't you remember?"

Right about then, Fern hollered, "Has anybody seen the turkey?"

"It's settin' next to the upside down cake," Sissy said. She's got the best memory in the family. Knows everybody's phone number by heart.

"And the dressin' and gravy?"

"Oh, here it is with the pickles and olives."

Barney didn't have no trouble at all findin' what he wanted.. He stepped on my feet and said, "Oops, I'm sorry. I was gonna go back to the head of the line for a napkin. Where is it?"

"Where's what?"

"The head of the line. Oh, I didn't see that meatloaf."

"Take half of mine, Barney, darlin'. I got the last piece when I got my yams."

"Yams? Did your sister bring 'em? She sure knows how to cook, don't she?"

"Well, by all means go back and get some if you think she's such a great cook. I don't see any of my carrot salad on your plate. What's the matter? Don't you like my carrot salad? Them green beans ain't mine either."

"Don't get excited, Myrtle. A green bean is a green bean as long as it's green. Your family can tell by lookin' at me that I love your cookin'. It's just good to eat what Grandma's other girls fix once in a while."

Of course, I know that. I just like to tease him. Besides, I don't have a jealous bone in my body. Well, I take that back. Maybe there's a tad of jealousy but I never let it show.

Anyways, where was I? Oh, yes, fillin' our plates. By the time we had finished and was ready to set down to eat, we'd passed by each other at least twice and had exchanged greetin's. So, I think Cousin Wade knew what he was doin'. He made us mingle more! And that's exactly what Grandma and Grandpa wanted us to do, bless their hearts.

Claudine, happy Thanksgivin', friend of mine. You're right at the top of my list of blessin's.

Love,
Myrtle, your friend forever

Lost Love

Dear Cora,

I'm writin' to tell you how much it meant to have you and Homer with me durin' the saddest days of my life. Just knowin' that you and Homer cared enough to rush here when you got word that Barney had died meant more to me than you will ever know.

You know, Cora, many times I could tell what he was thinkin' before he spoke. His smile made my heart tickle right up until the night of his stroke. At first, I wanted to die too, but I have the children and grandchildren to live for. And, I know that God will watch over me until it's my turn to leave this world and catch up with my Barney. My word, Cora, it seems like I have followed that man all my life. But that's okay. He never led me astray, you know.

But come to think of it, I've followed God most of my life too. God must have plans for me, but my life will never be the same. How can it be the same without him? Barney was such a special man and had been my soul mate for 49 years. How can I keep on livin' without him and ever be really happy again?

I just answered my own question, in my heart. It just this minute hit me like a bolt outta the blue. Remember me tellin' you about that Bristol car race Barney took me to? The car that looked like a box of Tide had wrecked and almost fell apart right before my very eyes but it never quit running. The driver just kept gettin' it and I said how he was settin' such a good example in life for us. Never give up. Keep on goin'. It was wonderful, Cora. I've got to remember that lesson and let God show me which way to go as I finish my race in life.

Cora, I hope you and Homer have many more years together. Love each other. Walk on the beach. Hold hands and hug when you pass in the hall. Those are the memories you'll cherish some day.

Mercy, Hon, I didn't mean to cry on your shoulder. I feel better now than I did when I started your letter. But, they say that's what friends are for. Thank you, sweet friend.

Write and let me know how you are. Take care of Homer.

Love, Myrtle,
your friend forever

Printed in the United States
26490LVS00005B/319-342